MAGIC & MERCY

STARRY HOLLOW WITCHES, BOOK 5

ANNABEL CHASE

RED PALM PRESS LLC

Magic & Mercy

Starry Hollow Witches, Book 5

By Annabel Chase

Sign up for my newsletter here http://eepurl.com/ctYNzf and like me on Facebook so you can find out about new releases.

Cover Design by Alchemy

✿ Created with Vellum

DEDICATION

Thanks to all those who serve others, whether that's as a mother, a soldier, a nurse, a waiter, or a butler.

Thank you also to my lovely reader, Irene Whitwell, for coming up with Bewitching Bites for the candy shop. You're on the map!

CHAPTER 1

MARLEY and I were summoned to the stables after school on Monday. On the walk across the grounds of Thornhold, my family's ancestral estate, my brain came up with twenty reasons why we might be in trouble, including a recent attempt to change Candle's color to pink. It was only a minor spell and I reversed the horse back to its normal white before anyone was the wiser, or so I believed. I planned to hold my tongue before admitting any wrongdoing, though.

Hyacinth Rose-Muldoon, my aunt and the family matriarch, was waiting out front when we arrived, managing to maintain her regal air amidst the haystacks and the smell of manure. Her teal kaftan was dotted with images of unicorn heads.

"No cats today?" I remarked. My aunt often favored clothing that reflected her familiar, the explosive snowflake named Precious.

She smoothed the front of her kaftan. "This one seemed appropriate to mark the occasion," she sniffed.

"And what occasion is that?" I asked.

"It isn't every day you get to present your great-niece with her very own unicorn."

Marley and I froze. Did she say what I thought she said?

"My own what?" Marley choked out the words.

"Unicorn, darling." My aunt regarded Marley. "It's my understanding that you're quite the skilled rider. I'm not one to let raw talent go to waste."

"Some kids get a used piano," I said.

"She's welcome to one of those, as well," my aunt said, as though I'd mentioned a pack of gum from the grocery store checkout line.

Marley had recently discovered a natural talent for piano, too. My daughter was full of surprises. I had to admit, it was thrilling for me to witness. There was no greater joy as a mother than watching your child thrive.

My aunt entered the stables and stopped in front of the first stall. "Magnificent, isn't she?"

The unicorn was breathtaking. With broad white shoulders, muscular legs, and a glowing silver horn, she was every little girl's fantasy come true.

"Maybe we should have discussed this ahead of time," I said.

"You object to such a fine creature?" Aunt Hyacinth asked, almost daring me.

"I don't object to the unicorn, of course." I wasn't a monster. "But maybe we should have discussed a payment plan. You can't just give a ten year old an expensive animal without a sense of responsibility."

"Mom, you know I'd never be irresponsible," Marley argued. "Especially not with a living creature."

I knew that much was true. Marley cared for everything from plants to frogs. She was far superior to me in that regard. I couldn't keep a cactus alive in the desert.

"That's not what I mean." I remembered my own childhood spent doing chores and odd jobs for pocket money. As soon as I was old enough to get a part-time job during school, I did. Then I got pregnant, of course, and all my plans dissolved.

"You've been given much and more since you've arrived in Starry Hollow," my aunt said. "A home, a position of respect, a nice car."

Guilt threatened to overwhelm me. "And I work hard to earn them, even retroactively." Not to mention that Rose Cottage had belonged to my parents and was rightfully mine. That sounded far too petty to say out loud, though. I *was* grateful for the tremendous start we'd been given here.

My aunt inclined her white-blond head. "What's your concern, darling?"

My concern was that my daughter would end up as spoiled and lazy as my cousin Florian, who had Aunt Hyacinth wrapped around his godlike finger. Admitting that was far too great a risk, though. I wasn't in the mood to become a toad for the rest of the day.

"I want Marley to learn the value of things," I said. "If you give her everything she could ever dream of in childhood without any elbow grease from her, what's left to strive for? There are lessons I want her to learn."

My aunt blew a dismissive breath. "Marley is a Rose, a descendant of the One True Witch. *Elbow grease*, as you so charmingly put it, is beneath her."

Marley clasped my hand. "Mom, you don't have to worry. I'm not going to become a spoiled brat, I promise. I want to learn to ride, and having a unicorn here is a great opportunity. Gives me more time to practice between lessons with Kelsey. It'll be an incentive to work harder."

"That was my thinking as well," my aunt said, satisfied with Marley's logic.

I found myself relenting. What was I going to do? Be the

kind of mother that deprives her daughter of her own unicorn? Ugh. Motherhood was a minefield.

"Fine," I said. "But you have to take care of her, too. You can't let the staff at Thornhold do all the dirty work."

"Deal," Marley said, doing a happy dance. It buoyed my heart to see her so upbeat. Her eyes had been opened to the cold reality of life and death at a young age, and it was often difficult to override that experience.

"Well chosen," my aunt said, clearly pleased that she'd won this round.

"Not much of a choice," I grumbled. I could understand my father's unwillingness to raise me within her sphere of influence. She was like a tractor beam, sucking in everything within range.

"Does she have a name?" Marley asked, her blue eyes shining with excitement. I couldn't blame her. I'd been excited over shiny unicorn stickers when I was ten. She had an actual unicorn.

"She's willing to be named by you," Aunt Hyacinth said. "That was part of the arrangement."

Marley stroked the unicorn's silky mane. "Firefly."

"A unicorn is not a pegasus, you know," Aunt Hyacinth said. "She cannot fly."

"I know the difference, Aunt Hyacinth," Marley said. "Thank you for your generous gift."

My aunt's mouth twisted in her version of a kind smile. "You're quite welcome, my dear. Perhaps we'll be attending your competitions soon."

No sooner did she finish speaking than Simon appeared with some fancy version of a rickshaw. Simon was Aunt Hyacinth's butler and had an uncanny knack for knowing exactly what she needed when she needed it. I was convinced there was magic at work, but Simon insisted that he was simply very good at his job. As soon as Aunt Hyacinth was settled inside, Simon lifted the arms and ran off in the direction of the main house, the wheels bouncing over the uneven ground.

"Simon must be in better shape than he seems," Marley observed.

I faced my daughter. "Confession time. You named her Firefly after the Joss Whedon show, didn't you?"

She gave me a coy look. "I don't know what you mean. I named her after the soft-bodied beetle with luminescent organs. The females are flightless, you know."

I touched the unicorn's glowing horn. "She's beautiful, Marley. You're a very lucky girl."

Marley leaned her head on my shoulder. "I belong to you, don't I? I was born lucky."

Without a jolt of magical caffeine, there was no way I could get through a morning of runecraft and crazy Hazel, or Crazel as Marley dubbed her one morning, causing me to spit out my cereal.

After walking Marley to school, I ducked into the Caffeinated Cauldron for a latte to keep me awake and alive. I tucked Prescott Peabody III, my aging Yorkshire terrier, inside my jacket so that only his disheveled head was visible. I wasn't sure about the pet policy, but I wasn't about to leave PP3 tied up outside. The old dog would keel over if I dared to leave him in an unfamiliar setting. No new tricks for my old dog included no new places.

I ordered a vanilla latte with a shot of talent.

"What's the talent for?" the barista asked.

"I have my first broomstick lesson tomorrow," I said. "I expect it to go well, but I can't be too careful." My luck had a way of deserting me in times of need.

"You don't have your license already?" the barista asked.

The elf was clearly new because everyone else in the coffee shop knew I was a transplant from the human world, New Jersey to be exact.

"This Rose is a late bloomer," I said.

"Ember, is that you? Why do you seem so...lumpy?" Linnea Rose-Muldoon stood beside me in all her resplendent glory. She was a sight to behold no matter what you were—human, paranormal, animal. They all basked in the glow of my cousin's ethereal beauty.

I turned to face her and PP3 forced a pathetic bark. "I'm taking the dog for a walk."

"Doesn't that require the dog to actually walk?" She brushed the dog's hair from his eyes. "Hello, sweetness."

"He's tired. What brings you here?" I asked. "Don't you have a top-of-the-line espresso machine at home?" Linnea ran Palmetto House, an inn that catered to Starry Hollow tourists.

"I do, but I'm busy with guests this week thanks to the Paranormal Estate Management Association's annual conference. I'm headed to the Wish Market for the second time this week for supplies."

"Oh, right. Aster mentioned the conference at our last tourism board meeting. It's a bunch of butlers descending on Starry Hollow, right?" I paused. "What's the collective noun for butlers?" There was a pride of lions. A troop of monkeys. An unkindness of ravens. I snapped my fingers. "How about a murder of butlers? Hmm. You should probably avoid that joke in front of your guests."

"I have to admit, butlers make the best guests," Linnea said. "They keep trying to wait on me instead. Creatures of habit."

"That must be a nice change for you," I said. Like me, Linnea was a single mother and always seemed to be working hard to keep her business afloat and her children happy.

"Absolutely," Linnea said. Her expression brightened. "You should come round for dinner tonight. They make wonderful dinner companions. So many enjoyable anecdotes from their estates." She hesitated. "I've already invited Rick."

"Really?" I was pleased, albeit surprised. Frederick Simms was a handsome minotaur who co-owned Paradise Found, the best garden center in town. I'd met him recently during an investigation of a dead elf found buried in a sand sculpture and thought that Rick might be a good match for my cousin. Linnea was the kind of beauty the average paranormal would deem unapproachable. Plus, she had the whole descendent of the One True Witch thing going on. That was intimidating all by itself.

"Does your mother know about Rick?" I queried. Aunt Hyacinth would *not* be pleased with the news that her daughter was dating a minotaur, even one as gregarious and attractive as Rick. My aunt preferred to keep romantic entanglements within the Silver Moon coven, not that she'd had much success. With the exception of Aster, who was married to a workaholic wizard, no one else in the family had found love within the coven.

Linnea pressed her rosebud lips together. "Not yet, although I'm sure her spies have reported sightings. We've tried to be discreet. I'll deal with Mother when I'm ready."

No doubt Aunt Hyacinth and her constant interferences served as an obstacle for even the most ardent of admirers.

"How about Bryn and Hudson?" I asked. "Have they met him yet?"

Linnea gave a quick shake of her white-blond head. "This dinner will be their first introduction. They don't know I'm dating him, so I thought a group setting would be best. I'm

7

hopeful that Wyatt doesn't get wind of it too soon. He'll be incorrigible."

I couldn't help but smile. Wyatt Nash was Linnea's ex-husband and the father of her two children. He was also the brother of my current...What did I call him? He was the brother of Sheriff Granger Nash, the grumpy werewolf I seemed to be dating at the moment, despite my best efforts to be alone. Although Marley liked the sheriff well enough, she seemed to be stuck on my boss, Alec Hale, as a potential love interest for me. She didn't know the extent of the damage I'd done to Alec recently with the opposite spell, though, and I had no plans to tell her. She'd be mortified and I didn't need to feel any more guilt than I already did.

"I need to get a move on," I said. "I'm already late for a runecraft lesson and you know how Hazel gets. What time should I be there tonight?"

"Seven o'clock," Linnea said. "Be sure to bring Marley. Her cousins are constantly asking for her."

A genuine smile came to my lips. I'd never had family around me growing up because my father had left Starry Hollow after my mother's death and hidden our identities so that we couldn't be found. As a result, I'd grown up alone in New Jersey with my father. The rift between the Rose siblings had prompted my father to leave the paranormal world far behind. He raised me as a human, cloaked our location, and suppressed my magic. It was only when I was in a life or death situation that my magic broke through and saved me. It also meant that the shield my father had created all those years ago had burst, allowing Aunt Hyacinth to find me. At first, I'd worried that he'd kept me hidden due to actual danger, but it seemed that it was simply a disagreement that resulted in lifelong estrangement. On occasion, I felt a pang of guilt for settling into Starry Hollow with

Marley, that I'd let my father down. Then, I would look at Marley and see how she was thriving here, and I knew that I wouldn't change a thing.

"Perfect," I said. "We'll be there."

CHAPTER 2

"You're late," Hazel said. The Mistress-of-Runecraft stood on the doorstep of Rose Cottage with her arms folded and a disapproving expression on her splotchy face. To be fair, she always wore the disapproving expression when she was with me.

"PP3 needs to pee first," I said, and set the dog on the ground. He circled a few bushes and trees before settling on a spot very close to Hazel's feet.

"Did you bring a drink for me?" Hazel asked, eyeing my takeaway cup.

"Sorry, I could only handle one cup with the dog." I opened the front door and Hazel nearly tripped over PP3 as he threaded his way through our feet to beat us inside. Even though he was old and ornery, he still liked to lead the pack.

I plopped onto the couch and kicked off my shoes. As much as I enjoyed the walk to and from school every day, it took a toll on my feet. I couldn't have normal soles—no siree —my arches had to rival the curve of a rainbow, resulting in chronic foot cramps. When Karl was alive, my amiable husband was tasked with rubbing my feet at the end of a long day. I still remembered the way his hands felt on my bare skin, strong and sure. I used to tease him about his sausage fingers, but they kneaded muscles like nobody's business. And he never complained about touching my misshapen feet, which I would've completely understood.

"What do you think you're doing?" Hazel asked, unpacking her bag on the table. She removed the Big Book of Scribbles, as well as a smaller drawstring bag of rune tiles.

"Making myself at home," I said. "Because I am."

"We have much to accomplish today," Hazel said. "Did you manage to complete your homework this time?"

I closed my eyes and groaned. "Yes, Miss Hazel."

"Let's see it then." She held out her hand and PP3 barked as though she was offering him a treat.

I dragged myself off the couch and went to hunt for the page of translations I'd finished late last night. I'd debated not doing the assignment just to annoy Hazel, but I worried that the crazed clown would seek vengeance through my aunt, so I acquiesced.

I opened and closed the drawers of the sideboard. "Where is it?"

"Where do you normally keep your homework?" Hazel asked. "Oh, that's right. You don't normally *do* any."

A thought occurred to me. I plucked the sheet from between the cushions of the couch and held up the wrinkled paper in triumph.

Hazel's nostrils flared. "How did it end up there?"

"I fell asleep toward the end," I said. "You can see right there where I trailed off." It resembled an EKG—the markings on the paper grew smaller and messier until they formed a wiggly line to the edge of the page.

"I don't know where Marley gets her acumen," Hazel said, placing the homework in her bag. "As a reward for actually completing an assignment, however messy, I've decided to focus on rune tiles today."

"To tell fortunes, or use as weapons?" I asked. I was happy with either option. Anything was better than another tour of the witchy alphabet.

"Weapons is a bit of a misdescription," Hazel said. She took the seat across from me and emptied the drawstring bag of tiles. "I thought it would be useful to learn a few defensive spells. You can carry the runes in your handbag for emergency purposes."

"Like a can of mace," I said, rubbing my hands together. "Sounds good to me." I angled my head. "Is this because of the incident at the ceramic factory?" Recently, I'd had to defend myself against a violent centaur in a room full of garden gnomes. Thanks to magic I'd learned from the Master-in-Familiar Arts, I was able to rally the gnomes and protect myself.

Hazel made a noise at the back of her throat. "Let's just say that trouble has a way of finding you, Ember. Your aunt would like to know that you can keep yourself safe without creating a spectacle."

Bells rang in my head. "So this wasn't your idea at all! You don't care if I can defend myself with runes."

Hazel braided her stubby fingers. "Don't be ridiculous. Of course I care."

"Then why not teach me defensive runes before now?" I challenged her.

"Because lessons should be taught in a certain order and in a certain way," she snapped. "Not at the pleasure of her ladyship."

Uh oh. Hazel was clearly bent out of shape by my aunt's request. "It's okay, Hazel. Your head won't explode because you taught a lesson out of order. The fabric of the universe will remain intact. Promise."

Hazel struggled to hold her tongue. "Were you this challenging in school?"

I pretended to examine my nails. "Mrs. Killarney said I was an absolute joy to have in class."

"One teacher in all your years of education is hardly a ringing endorsement."

"Plus, I wasn't her student," I said. "I was in the classroom next door, but I was so loud, she claimed she could hear me even when I sneezed."

Hazel rolled her eyes. "Why does this news not surprise me? I'm going to start with this tile here." She set the small square in front of me. The marking was in the shape of a crooked 'H'.

"Aw, that's so sweet. 'H' for Hazel," I said, picking up the tile to study it. She should have started with 'C' for Crazel.

"This rune carries many possibilities," Hazel said. "In fortune telling, it represents difficult changes ahead and the need to embrace them rather than fear them."

I knew a certain vampire that could benefit from this particular rune.

"In magic, it represents the idea of transformation," Hazel continued.

"Are we talking ugly duckling into beautiful swan type transformations?" I queried. I had a small roll of fat around my stomach that could do with a transformative spell.

"If that transformation would protect you from harm, then I guess so," Hazel said. "The meaning is flexible, depending on your needs. I was thinking more along the lines of invisibility, for your purposes."

My breathing hitched. "This rune can make me invisible?"

She nodded. "If you perform the spell correctly, then yes."

I traced the carving of the 'H' with my index finger. "Why not just astral project like Marigold taught me?" Marigold was the Mistress-of-Psychic Skills and only slightly less crazy than Hazel.

"Because astral projection doesn't render you invisible," Hazel said. "In fact, it leaves you in a vulnerable state with your physical body in one place and your consciousness running around somewhere else. I wouldn't recommend it for defensive purposes."

"I won't tell Marigold that if you won't," I said. It wouldn't surprise me to learn that the two witches were competitive when it came to their areas of expertise. One was as uptight as the other.

"Take the rune and press into the palm of your hand," Hazel instructed.

"Like I'm branding myself?"

Her brow wrinkled. "You do have a violent streak, don't you?"

"It was an innocent question."

"No, not like you're branding yourself. Simply so the rune is secure and doesn't fall to the ground. You lose the rune, you lose your chance to do magic."

"What if I have my wand?" I countered.

Hazel gave an exasperated sigh. "An assailant can see a wand coming a mile away. A rune is more difficult to detect. You can take someone by surprise, which could mean the difference between life and death."

I tapped the corner of the rune on the table, thinking. "Why was I able to use magic without any objects back in New Jersey?" Granted, it was only one time, but I didn't have a wand or runes then. Hell, I didn't even know magic was real.

Hazel placed a hand over mine to stop the tapping. "Please don't do that. You'll damage the rune." When I stopped tapping, she continued. "You're talking about the rain?"

I nodded. When violent mobster Jimmy 'the Lighter' Litano came after me, I somehow summoned the strength of Mother Nature to save myself. He'd set my car on fire and I'd brought down a rainstorm to douse the flames. It was the whole reason I was in Starry Hollow now.

"You were under tremendous stress," Hazel said. "And you're a Rose, don't forget. Your family has a way of manifesting magic that dwarfs your average coven witch."

"So why couldn't I do that again?" I asked. "Why the runes and the wand?"

Hazel leaned back in her chair. "I don't know. Why did you rely on a wand to bring the ceramic garden gnomes to life? Why not summon a bolt of lightning instead?"

I drummed my fingers on the table. "In the ceramics factory, I was thinking about how to defend myself. With Jimmy, I didn't think at all. I just reacted."

"You have more control with a wand or a rune," Hazel said. "You were lucky with the storm you summoned. You could've killed an innocent person or yourself in the process. Runes and your wand—those are tools you use to focus your powers until you're advanced enough to do without them. Even your cousins favor their wands, and they're more than capable of practicing magic without them."

Yes, I'd seen my cousins in action against Jimmy the Lighter. They were a formidable trio. If I could develop my magic to that level, I'd never worry about my safety again.

I touched the rune again. "Congratulations, Hazel. You've convinced me. Now, how do I make myself invisible?"

Marley and I stood on the front step of Palmetto House. From the blue wrought iron balconies to the Silver Moon flag that waved in the breeze, the beautiful building never failed to impress me. Linnea always had a fresh batch of flowers woven into the scalloped wrought iron, like a tactile tapestry.

"Now, Marley," I said. "Rick is a fairly big guy with horns, but you don't need to be intimidated. He's incredibly nice."

Marley gave me an exasperated look. "I've seen him at the beach, remember? And since when would I be intimidated by someone based on his looks? That's not the daughter you've raised. I only judge books by their covers."

The front door clicked open.

"Welcome to Palmetto House," an unfamiliar man greeted us.

"Um, thank you," I said. "Where's Linnea?"

"The lady of the house is making final preparations in the kitchen. Do come in."

Marley and I entered the main living area and I took a moment to admire the parquet floor and traditional throw rugs. The fireplace was decorated with a string of fairy lights that reflected the silver of the marble. Unsurprisingly, my cousin had excellent taste.

"Let me guess," I said. "You're here for the butler conference."

The man smiled at me. "I believe you mean PEMA, the Paranormal Estate Management Association conference. How do you do? My name is Bates. This is my third year attending, but my first time staying at Palmetto House. It's a fine establishment. Very fine, indeed."

Marley zeroed in on the man's hands. "Do you always wear white gloves?"

I understood the implication. Bates was not on duty while at the conference. Why bother with the white glove treatment?

Bates laughed softly. "Habit, miss. My hands would feel naked without my gloves after all these years. I've even been known to wear them to the beach."

"That must make for some sweaty palms," Marley said.

"Perhaps," he said, "but as a household manager, our motto is never let them see you sweat."

"I'm pretty sure that motto has been taken," I said. By a deodorant company.

Linnea glided into the room, her white-blond hair in a tight braid and a serene smile on her face. She seemed genuinely pleased to have company tonight. "So glad the two of you are here. Everyone else is in the dining room." She nudged Bates. "What did I tell you about answering the door? You don't work for Palmetto House, Bates. You're a guest. You need to act like one."

A blush crept into the older man's cheeks. "Again, a creature of habit. I find it difficult to do nothing."

Linnea took him by the shoulders and guided him toward the dining room. "You won't be doing nothing. You'll be getting to know the other guests and showing everyone how marvelous you are."

Marley and I exchanged amused looks. Butlers weren't so different from mothers.

The dining room was already lively when we arrived. Bryn and Hudson were at opposite ends of the table, engaged in their usual sibling banter.

"I separated them at the table," Linnea said, "but they still find a way to aggravate each other from a distance." She shrugged her narrow shoulders. "Teenagers. What can you do?"

Bates nodded sagely. "I completely understand. I've served my estate through quite a few teenagers."

"And were they as unruly as mine?" Linnea asked.

"Oh, my dear. You should thank your lucky stars that the Goddess of the Moon blessed you with such wonderful offspring. You don't want to hear the scenes I've witnessed."

I took a seat beside another stranger. He was younger

than Bates, with straight, dark hair and a hint of Asian ancestry.

"Ember, Marley," Linnea said. "I'd like you to meet Trevor Jenkins, another guest of the inn."

Jenkins stood to shake my hand. "A pleasure." He gave Marley a curt nod. "Young Miss."

"You're a butler, too?" Marley asked.

"That's right," Jenkins replied. "I work for Lawrence Stanhope."

"Marley, this other gentleman is Rick," I said. "He co-owns Paradise Found, that cool garden center I told you about."

Marley's face lit up. "I'd love to see it sometime. Mom says you have a maze. I love mazes."

"We've designed the entire outdoor portion of the garden center as a maze," Rick said. "My business partner thought it was a clever idea because I'm a minotaur."

Marley's brow furrowed. "You don't have any horns or a bull face. Are there minotaur shifters?"

Rick smiled indulgently. "I chose a human form for dinner tonight. I guess we're sort of like shifters. Minotaurs who want to shift to a human form have to use magic. We can't shift at will like your cousins here." He tilted his head toward Bryn.

"How do you use magic if you're a minotaur?" Marley asked. "Do you pay someone to make you a custom potion?"

Rick's brown eyes widened. "I have a feeling you're going to follow in your mother's inquisitive footsteps."

"It's nice that you said 'inquisitive' instead of 'nosy,'" I interjected.

"I don't think so," Marley said matter-of-factly. "I'm more interested in the magical sciences. I'll decide next year, once my magic manifests."

Inwardly, I groaned. Marley was sure she'd come into her magic at eleven like most witches. There was a chance, however, that she would inherit her father's human genes and develop no magic at all. She seemed to think that because I was a descendent of the One True Witch that my magic would be strong enough to overpower her father's DNA. It didn't work for Linnea, though, so I had my doubts.

"I was employed by the estate where a wizard once lived," Bates said. "A lovely chap, also very interested in the magical sciences. He had an entire room devoted to potions. Called it the mixology room, which, I admit, is not very clever."

Marley's excitement was palpable. "The whole room? Like a craft room?"

"Bigger," Bates replied. "The size of a laboratory."

"You said you were employed by the estate rather than by the wizard," I said. "What do you mean by that?"

"The butler is attached to the home rather than the paranormal who lives there," Bates explained. "When the home changes hands for any reason, I remain at Brigadoon. I don't leave to join the family elsewhere. I serve the estate first and foremost."

"Exactly," Jenkins said. "Most paranormals think we work for the owner of the home. That's why I always say I work for Mr. Stanhope. Makes it easier."

"I've heard of the Stanhopes," Bates said. "I met one of their butlers here last year. A gent by the name of Higgins."

Jenkins took a sip from his water goblet. "Yes. Higgins works for the estate owned by Mr. Stanhope's sister, Lottie. This is my first year attending the conference. Mr. Stanhope heard such good things about it from his sister that he decided it would be worth doing without me for a few days."

"What do they do when you're gone?" I asked. "Do they have substitute butlers?"

I tried to imagine Aunt Hyacinth coping without Simon. It wouldn't surprise me in the least to learn that the conference was held in Starry Hollow so that Simon could still resume his duties in the evenings upon his return.

"The master of Brigadoon travels whilst I attend," Bates said. "He has a home in St. Tropez and separate household staff to attend to him there."

I whistled. "Must be nice."

"Mr. Stanhope is staying with extended family in England," Jenkins said. "His sister recently died and the family has been in mourning."

"That's a shame," Linnea said. "Were they close?" She looked from Hudson to Bryn. "Please say they were close."

"I would say they were cordial," Jenkins said. "I look forward to seeing Higgins tomorrow to pay my respects."

"Do you think Higgins will be here this year?" I asked.

"Like Bates said, the butler remains with the estate," Jenkins said. "Higgins is here for the house, not so much the family that occupies it."

"Will the estate change hands?" Marley asked. "Maybe a new family will move in, one with small kids."

"I believe the estate has been left to Lottie's adult daughter, Laura. She has her own home, Nightingale, so I'm not sure what her intentions are regarding her late mother's estate."

"What's it like becoming witch at such a late stage?" Bates asked. He immediately realized how his question sounded. "Apologies, I meant a late stage for a magic user, not to suggest you're as old and decrepit as me."

"I knew what you meant, Bates. As it happens, I'll be engaged in my first broomstick lesson tomorrow. It's the first step toward my license, so knock wood for me."

"And where will this moment in history take place?" Rick asked. "Any chance I can buy a ticket?"

I swallowed the rest of my wine. "Bystanders probably aren't safe. I enjoyed flying as part of the local broomstick tour, but doing it on my own will be an entirely different experience."

"Don't sell yourself short," Linnea said. "You are a Rose, after all. Flying is in our blood."

I noticed Marley's expression shift. "What's wrong, Marley?

She fiddled with her cutlery. "Maybe you're right and I'll inherit more of Dad's genes. I'm afraid of heights. If flying is in the Rose genes, maybe that means I don't have the right ones." Her voice cracked. "So I won't come into my magic next year."

I gave her arm a soft squeeze. "Let's not worry about that right now, okay? It's nothing we can control. And we don't worry about things that we can't control, do we?" We learned that lesson the hard way.

"Your mother's right," Linnea said. "It's best to surrender to what is, rather than what you wish it would be."

Hudson snorted. "Mom, you're so profound."

Linnea narrowed her eyes at her son. "Save your sarcasm for dessert. It goes down easier with whipped cream."

"Everything goes down easier with whipped cream," Bates said cheerfully. "I had one young master who insisted his broccoli be bathed in it before he would agree to eat it."

Hudson's head jerked toward his mother. "Can we try that?"

"Absolutely not," Linnea replied.

Marley smiled at me. "Would you try it with brussel sprouts?"

"You could deep fry them or coat them in chocolate," I said. "Still not happening."

Marley addressed the rest of the table. "And she thinks *I'm* the picky eater."

"Did you tell your cousins about your gift from Aunt Hyacinth?" I asked.

"A unicorn," Marley said.

Linnea's fork hovered above her plate. "And you agreed?"

"I thought it best not to look a gift unicorn in the mouth," I replied.

"Tread carefully," Linnea warned. "Most of the time, Mother means well. Once in a blood moon, however, she means something else entirely. You don't want to wake up one day and discover she owns you."

"We're already indebted to her," I said. The cottage, the job, the car—my aunt wasn't wrong to mention those things.

Linnea flashed a bright smile, clearly intended to put everyone at ease. "Every loving family has its thorns, especially the Roses. Just be careful, Ember."

My heart thumped against my chest. "I will."

CHAPTER 3

THE NEXT MORNING, I dragged myself to the offices of *Vox Populi*, the weekly paper owned by my aunt and my place of employment. I dreaded coming to work, knowing that Alec wouldn't be here. The editor-in-chief had been away for two weeks now. Although he kept in contact with Tanya, the office manager, he didn't reach out to me. I deserved it, not that he realized that. I'd recently cast a spell on him that made him act the opposite of his normal personality. With the misguided flick of a wand, he was the Alec Hale he was meant to be — fun-loving, open, and honest. Not the incommunicative vampire we were used to. The one who refused to call me by first name in order to maintain emotional distance. He was so mortified after returning to his stoic state that he left town without a word to anyone except Tonya.

"Here before ten? What's the occasion—an early nail appointment?" Bentley Smith, my co-worker and resident pain in my butt, delighted in giving me a hard time whenever possible.

I dropped into the chair beside him. "Why so cranky? Did your girlfriend finally realize she was dating *you?*"

Bentley stiffened. "Meadow and I are still going strong, thank you." Bentley and Meadow met on MagicMirror, a paranormal social media site. They'd gotten a rocky start thanks to a magical parasite, but seemed to have overcome their unfortunate beginning.

"Tonya said you needed me here to cover a story. So I'm here. I had to push my broomstick training back to late afternoon. Aunt Hyacinth was none too pleased about it, I'll have you know." As the *de facto* leader in Starry Hollow, my aunt could wield her power with a whisper or a hurricane, depending on her mood.

"She'll be pleased when she knows which story you're covering," Bentley said. "After all, her beloved right hand is involved."

My antenna went up. "Simon?"

He touched the tip of his long, slightly upturned nose. "You've got it. It's the annual butler conference."

Ugh. "You want me to cover the butler conference?" I couldn't think of anything less interesting. Maybe a paint-drying convention or an in-depth discussion on the invention of the wiffleball bat. "Why don't you cover it?"

Bentley smirked. "You're still the new fish, Rose, and you seem out-of-favor with our fearless leader at the moment, so I'm taking the opportunity…"

"To be a complete turd?" I finished for him. "You're not the boss of me, Bentley." I knew I sounded like a petulant child, but Bentley seemed to bring that out in me. He was like the brother I never wanted.

Tonya fluttered over to intervene. "I'm sorry, Ember. Alec did leave him in charge of assignments in his absence. If Bentley wants you to cover the conference, I'm afraid you must."

I gritted my teeth. I debated invoking the wrath of Aunt Hyacinth, but decided this particular argument didn't warrant her involvement. I'd save that card for a rainy day. "Fine. I'll do it. Where is it and what time?"

Bentley inclined his head toward the office manager. "Tanya will provide the details. Make sure you pay attention. You wouldn't want to miss anything earth-shattering."

I flicked his arm with my pen.

"Ouch," he yelled, and rubbed the sore spot on his arm. "I forget how violent they raise your kind in New Jersey."

"If you think that's violent…"

Tonya dropped a slip of paper onto my desk. "Please do not list all of the ways in which you could have been more violent," she said. "I don't need to be breaking up a brawl while Alec is still away."

Instinctively, my gaze drifted to the back of the office, where Alec's private office was nestled in the corner. "Any word?" I asked quietly.

"I'm sure he'll be back very soon," she responded in an equally quiet voice.

"I hope he's enjoying himself, wherever he is," Bentley said. "I can't remember the last time he took a holiday. It's completely out of character."

"I think it's high time," Tanya said. "He'll work himself into an early grave if he doesn't slow down." She paused, thinking. "I suppose, as a vampire, he's done the early grave part already, hasn't he?"

I didn't want to contemplate how Alec might be enjoying himself right now, especially in light of the fact that none of the options included me.

"What happened to make him leave in the first place?" Bentley asked. "I've been dying to know. He'd been acting so strangely just before he left. Karaoke in a bar?" He whistled. "By the gods, do I wish I could've seen that performance."

"It was incredible," I admitted, but I refused to say anything more on the subject. I wasn't about to tell Bentley that I was the reason Alec left. That we'd nearly engaged in carnal relations while Alec was under the opposite spell and that the buttoned-up vampire was probably still reeling from the aftereffects. He'd been so careful to keep his distance from me and I'd blown his comfort zone to smithereens with a single flick of my wand.

"Never you mind, Bentley," Tonya said. "Your job is to keep the paper ticking along, not writing a gossip column about your boss."

Bentley began tapping away on his keyboard. "Not to worry, Tonya. I'm working on a more important story than the butler conference. Alec is going to be very pleased when he returns."

I highly doubted that, since Alec Hale was never very pleased about anything.

I glanced at the paperwork on my desk. "Wait. The conference started twenty minutes ago."

Bentley gave me a look of mock surprise. "You don't say? You'd better hurry then. Don't want to miss any of the juicy bits. Maybe you can show us best practices for polishing the silver when you get back."

I punched his arm as I rose to my feet. He winced and rubbed the sore spot.

"I'll check in with you later, Tonya," I said. "If you hear from Alec, will you let me know?"

Tonya nodded. "Of course, dear. Good luck today."

"Thanks," I said, although it wasn't luck I needed. It was the ability to liven up the most boring day possible.

The Starry Hollow Convention Center was not what I was expecting. Although the large lobby appeared normal, the surrounding conference rooms were arranged like the rooms of a grand estate. A directory board hovered in the middle of the lobby, detailing the schedule for the day. Registration had taken place in the lobby an hour ago. There was a first timer's orientation in the Billiard Room. The welcome reception took place in the Main Parlor Room. According to the clock, that was where I would find the attendees right now. My curiosity piqued, I scanned the remainder of the schedule. There were a few sessions to choose from in each timeslot. Next offerings were: Of Human Bondage: The Day in the Life of a Household Manager; Eleven Ways Every Butler Can Increase Their Productivity; and From Ancestral Estate to McMansion: A Reversal of Fortune. There were several vendors scheduled to speak as well. Cleaning companies, golf course designers, gardening experts, a one-on-one with a life coach. Tomorrow was even better. A morning of trust exercises, then more lectures: Butlering Demystified; Butler Basics; Driving Miss Daisy: Pitfalls to Avoid; The House You Built: A Blueprint for Effective Household Management; and Five Reasons Your Staff Doesn't Respect You and How to Fix It.

This was a jam-packed schedule. I could understand why it was such a popular conference. Before I could make a move toward the welcome reception, a man in black tails and a crisp white shirt intercepted me.

"Can I help you, miss? You look lost," he said.

"I'm covering the conference for the local paper, *Vox Populi*," I said. "I'm running a bit late. Do you know where the Main Parlor Room is?"

He offered his arm. "Right this way. I happen to be heading there myself. I tried to use the restroom closest to the conference room, but the door was locked, so I had to hurry to this end. I'll need to alert management once the reception is over."

Entering the welcome reception was like entering the grand foyer of Versailles. The room itself was enormous, designed to resemble the entryway of an estate that made Thornhold look like a crab shack. I was glad Aunt Hyacinth wasn't here. She'd probably run directly to a local architect to rectify the inadequacy.

The butlers stood in rows, listening to the speaker. It was like walking into a room of attentive penguins.

"Why aren't there any women?" I asked my helpful companion.

"If you look closely, there are a few here," he said. "The profession is still heavily dominated by men, though."

"Who's speaking?" I whispered. A man stood facing the penguins, addressing the crowd.

"That's Belvedere," he said. "He's this year's president of the association. The president always gives the welcoming address."

I typed notes on my phone as I listened. I wasn't really sure what the pertinent information to convey was. Did readers care about changes in the world of estate management? For the most part, paranormals were no different from people—they wanted to live vicariously through those whose lives seemed much more glamorous. Clearly, the owners of these estates lived such lives.

I scanned the matching ensembles for Simon. He'd be a good butler to attach myself to if I could manage it. It helped that I also happened to be fond of him.

While searching the crowd, I spotted Jenkins and Bates. I gave a small wave, but only Bates noticed me. He offered a friendly nod in return. The room was so quiet that I hoped no one had a rumbling stomach, or worse, because the sound would definitely echo.

As the president began his closing remarks, the door flew open and a man stumbled in, clutching his stomach. His white shirt was stained red and he dripped a trail of blood as he staggered across the floor. No one screamed. The unflappable butlers remained eerily calm as the man fell to the floor and promptly died.

"Someone call a healer," a voice shouted.

"A healer can't resuscitate the dead," someone else replied.

"Help him!"

In the blink of an eye, the body was completely surrounded. I pushed my way through the crowd and everyone moved politely aside as I did so. Their manners were impeccable, even in a crisis.

I kneeled beside the body and checked for a pulse. Nothing.

"Miss Rose, whatever are you doing here?"

I craned my neck to see Simon behind me. "What does it look like? Finding trouble, just like I usually do."

Simon appeared concerned. "Your aunt will be most displeased."

"With which part?" I asked. "The fact that I'm on the scene, or the fact that Starry Hollow's body count is piling up faster than the number of disappointing Will Smith movies?"

"Both, I'm afraid." Simon dabbed away the beads of sweat on his forehead with a neatly pressed handkerchief and I noticed several other butlers doing the same.

I stood and dusted off my hands. Time to get loud. "Everyone stand back and give us space," I demanded. "Law enforcement is on the way." Or would be, as soon as I made the call. Sometimes it was handy to have the sheriff on speed dial.

Simon clucked his tongue. "Yet one more thing my mistress will object to."

"The sheriff has to investigate," I said. "It's his job." As I finished my sentence, I glanced at a small spot on Simon's shirt. "Simon, is that…blood?"

He looked down at his white shirt. "Hmm. I believe it is."

"Simon has blood on his shirt!" someone yelled.

"Simon killed him!"

Simon's eyes met mine and I saw the fear and panic reflected there.

Sweet baby Elvis. What had I done?

CHAPTER 4

I RECOGNIZED the familiar swagger of Sheriff Granger Nash as he entered the convention center. I watched as his gaze darted from left to right, quickly assessing the scene. Behind him, Deputy Bolan struggled to keep up with the werewolf's longer strides. The leprechaun tried to make his movements seem effortless, but the pink cheeks and labored breathing betrayed him.

Deputy Bolan scowled when he noticed me beside the body. "You again?" He elbowed the sheriff. "Look, boss. Bad Penny is here."

I shot the leprechaun a quizzical look. "Bad Penny? That sounds like a stripper name."

The sheriff chuckled. "That's what they call you down at my office. You always turn up when something horrible happens."

"Yeah," Deputy Bolan chimed in. "You're bad luck, pure and simple."

"Well, that's just insulting," I said. "I'm here covering the conference for *Vox Populi*. I can't help it if one butler decided to take a stab at another. It's nothing to do with me."

"So you're saying the butler did it?" the sheriff quipped.

"Oh, hilarious," I said. "I'm sure we'll only hear that joke about a hundred more times before the case is closed."

"Sheriff, we're so relieved you're here," Simon said, unusually ruffled. "The entire conference is in chaos."

The sheriff blinked as he glanced around the calm, quiet room. "You and I have a different understanding of chaos."

"This butler has blood on his shirt," a man said. I recognized Belvedere, the president of the association.

The sheriff looked down at the spot on Simon's shirt. "So he does." He cocked his head. "Simon, anything you can tell us about what happened? Do you know this butler's name?"

"His name is Higgins, sir," Simon said. "I met him at dinner last night. A number of us got together for a meal and this butler was a member of our party."

"Ooh. A night out?" I taunted him. "I bet Aunt Hyacinth wasn't happy about that."

Simon wore a mask of tolerance. "My mistress was taken care of before I left. I would never leave her needs unmet."

I sure hoped he was talking about her evening cocktail.

"You said you met him for the first time last night?" the sheriff asked, seeking clarification.

Simon stared down at the body. "Yes, sir. I knew Jeeves and Stevens from last year's conference. I believe Higgins tailed along because they were staying in the same hotel."

"And which hotel is that?" the deputy asked.

"The Gryphon," Simon replied.

"Is that where you had dinner?" I asked. "At the hotel restaurant?"

The sheriff shot me a look. "We're perfectly capable of handling the investigation, Rose."

"Since when?" I shot back.

"As a matter fact, we had dinner at the Flying Pig. It offers an excellent view of the pier." Simon removed another neatly folded handkerchief from his jacket pocket and carefully dabbed his brow with it.

"How many of those do you carry around at a pop?" I asked.

Deputy Bolan blew a raspberry. "If you're going to ask questions, why not limit them to relevant ones only?"

"Anyone else attend this dinner?" the sheriff asked. "I'll need a list of names."

Simon gave a crisp nod. "Of course, sir. Whatever you need, I am at your disposal."

"What about the blood?" Belvedere persisted, pointing to Simon's shirt. "You should at least test it to see if it belongs to Higgins."

"Even if it does, that doesn't prove he killed him," I said. Belvedere was rubbing me the wrong way. He seemed a little too eager to pin the murder on Simon, probably because he didn't want the situation to taint his organization. "The guy was dripping blood everywhere. It's possible a little drop landed on Simon's shirt."

"Deputy Bolan, please secure the area where there's evidence of blood," the sheriff said, pointing to the trail on the floor.

"Yes, Sheriff." The leprechaun set to work and the sheriff returned his attention to Simon.

"What did you talk about at dinner?" he asked. "Any controversial topics? Any arguments?"

"Dear me, no," Simon replied. "We're trained to avoid such unpleasantness. That's why butlers typically make excellent company even when we're off duty."

"I have to agree," I said. "I met a couple for dinner at Linnea's last night and they were delightful."

"Delightful or not, we need to clear all these butlers out of here," the sheriff said. "Deputy, once you've secured the area, take down names and any witness statements before dispersing the crowd."

The leprechaun stood and faced the room. There was no way he could handle this on his own. They'd be here all day.

"I can help," I said. I knew the deputy wouldn't like it, but he was too smart to ignore the fact that he needed assistance.

Deputy Bolan flinched. "I'll allow it today," he said. "But don't think it gives you a license to do my job whenever you feel like it."

"I wouldn't dream of it," I said. "My dance card is full enough as it is."

"Simon, don't go anywhere," the sheriff instructed. "I'm going to need you to come down to the office with me when we're finished here."

"Oh, come on, Granger," I objected.

The sheriff gave me a sharp look. "It's Sheriff Nash when I'm working, Miss Rose."

"Right. Sorry," I mumbled. He'd been encouraging me to call him Granger, and now that I made the effort, he gave me the smackdown. Ugh. We'd never get this relationship right.

I didn't miss the hint of a smile on Deputy Bolan's tiny face.

While the sheriff studied the evidence on and around the body, the deputy and I worked in tandem to organize the butlers into groups. Those that saw something, and those that did not. Obviously, I was tasked with handling the oblivious, which consisted mostly of the butlers at the back of the room. I made a list of names, contact details, and times of arrival, and let them go.

"Sheriff Nash, thank the gods." A curvaceous woman hurried into the room, her ample bottom swinging from side to side. Behind her was a petite pixie, her wings moving so quickly that they were almost invisible. "I just received word and got here as soon as I could."

"No need to panic. We have everything under control, Tish," the sheriff said.

The sheriff knew this buxom woman called Tish?

"Tish Wells is the manager of the convention center," Simon whispered, noting my confusion.

"This is a catastrophe," she said, surveying the room. "The town will lose money on this conference if we have to cancel the remainder of it, not to mention the taint of a *murder*."

"You can just delay it," I said. "Many of the butlers won't be allowed to leave town until the case is resolved. If they're stuck here, they may as well continue the conference."

She brightened. "An excellent point. The show must go on." She faced the pixie. "Make a note, Niamh. Send a message to all the butlers with a revised schedule attached. Butlers adore schedules."

"Quite true, Miss Wells," Simon said.

Tish stroked her chin. "Yes, we actually have a two-day gap between the end of this conference and the start of the next. It's entirely possible to carry on. Miss Rose, I'm so grateful for your suggestion."

I didn't ask how she knew my name since it seemed to be a common occurrence. I was the long-lost Rose child, a novelty act.

"Occasionally, I have a good idea," I said. "Try not to let word get out, though. The less competent I appear, the more I'm able to accomplish." I winked at her.

"Make a note, Niamh. Miss Rose has a sense of humor." Tish moved to stand beside the sheriff. "Cause of death?"

"Looks like stab wounds," the sheriff said. He held up a corkscrew. "Someone tried to open him up like a fine bottle of wine."

I winced at the gruesome sight. "That's awful."

"Sure is. The worst part is that there were multiple stab

wounds until the murderer decided to twist to this into his gut. My guess is that was the deathblow."

I closed my eyes, unwilling to see the gory details on the corkscrew itself.

"That looks like one of the corkscrews from our Wine Cellar Room," Tish said.

"I noticed that room on the convention center map," I said. It was located just to the right of the lobby, not far from the restrooms.

The sheriff gave me an appraising look. "Because it had the word 'wine' in it?"

"Because there was an interesting session there in the afternoon," I countered.

"I'll have to take this one to the lab," the sheriff said to Tish. "I imagine you have extras."

"Of course, Sheriff." Tish lowered her voice. "I may need to cancel drinks tonight if I need to prepare for tomorrow's revised schedule."

Drinks? I looked from Tish to Sheriff Nash.

"It's a community thing, Rose," the sheriff said, seemingly reading my thoughts. "A chamber of commerce event with business leaders."

"You're not a business leader," I pointed out.

"Ta-ta for now," Tish said. "We'll talk later, yes?"

The sheriff nodded as Tish and Niamh left the scene.

"Do I detect a little jealousy?" the sheriff asked, barely suppressing a grin.

I poked him with my elbow. "Of what? She's like a hundred years older than me."

He chuckled. "A little jealousy is nice, Rose. Strokes the ego. And you're right, she's probably a good hundred years older than you."

"Seriously?" I'd been kidding about the age difference.

"What is she?" Tish had too much color in her cheeks to be a member of the undead community.

"A succubus," the deputy interjected, appearing incredibly pleased to share this information with me.

"The type of paranormal that's all about sex as food?" I queried.

"In a nutshell," the deputy said, pleased with his revelation.

I cast a sidelong glance at the sheriff. "And how often do you and Tish meet up for…drinks?"

The sheriff didn't bother to hide his amusement. "Once a month, when the group gets together at the Wishing Well. You know the Wishing Well. You and I have had a few drinks there together, too, as I recall."

"Not the kind of drinks you probably have with *her*," I said pointedly.

"As adorable as this development is," the sheriff said, kneeling beside Higgins, "I need to finish up here so we can transport the body."

"Deputy Bolan, if you're finished with the witness statements, you can escort Simon to my office for questioning."

I'd need to let Aunt Hyacinth know about Simon without tipping off the sheriff. He'd be irritated if he knew I ratted him out since he viewed my aunt as an obstacle at the best of times.

"Well, the good news is that the butlers will need to stay in town until the case is closed," I said.

The sheriff frowned. "How is that good news?"

"They need to stay at local hotels and eat at restaurants," I said. "That's revenue for Starry Hollow."

The sheriff shook his head. "That sounds like your aunt talking. There are more important things than money, Rose."

"I know that," I replied indignantly. I could say that with

the confidence of someone who grew up with not very much of it. "I'm just trying to think of the bright side."

The sheriff looked over his shoulder at the body. "Somebody died a horrible death today, Rose. I certainly can't see the bright side of that."

"Does Mother know?" Florian asked, aghast.

"She does now," I said. "Poor Simon. I shouldn't have drawn attention to the blood."

We stood in the middle of Adelaide Rose-Brixham Park, preparing for my broomstick lesson. He seemed an unlikely teacher, given that, in the time we'd been in Starry Hollow, I'd never once seen him straddle a broomstick.

"Nice shirt," Florian said, glancing down as I removed my cloak. "Maybe a little too on-the-nose for today's lesson."

I looked at my green T-shirt and smiled. *Broom Hair, Don't Care* was emblazoned across my chest, along with the silhouette image of a witch riding a broomstick. "Ha! I swear it wasn't on purpose. Marley saw it in a shop and insisted I buy it."

"It's cute. I like the ones for fairies that say things like *Glitterati* in sparkly letters."

"You just like an excuse to ogle their chests," I said. "Now explain to me again why you're the one in charge of my broomstick lesson?"

"I was a master broomstickman in my youth," he boasted. If it were anybody else making such a claim, I'd laugh. Knowing Florian, however, he probably mastered the broomstick before he was old enough to walk. My cousins were blessed by good fortune in every respect.

"Let me guess," I said. "You were a gold medalist in broomstick flying in the coven Olympics."

Florian pointed the handle of the broomstick at me. "I can

tell by your New Jersey tone that you're being sarcastic, but the truth is that I did medal in the Broomstick Challenges when I attended the Black Cloak Academy," Florian said. "And, for the record, there's no such thing as a coven Olympics."

"Well, maybe there ought to be," I said. "It would be much cooler than Quidditch. That game makes no sense whatsoever."

He squinted. "You're using that vocabulary again that escapes me."

"It's called the wizarding world of Harry Potter," I said haughtily. "It wouldn't kill you to crack open a book every now and again."

"Yes, yes, we all know how you and Marley enjoy your literature. I'm not a complete heathen. I enjoy a good history book now and again."

At the mention of history books, my thoughts immediately went to Delphine, the town librarian. Delphine Winter was a witch in the coven with a mad crush on Florian, not that he had any clue. Delphine was smart and pretty, but painfully shy; definitely not the type to catch Florian's attention. He tended to prefer the effortless ones. He also tended to avoid witches completely because he knew it was his mother's preference that he date within the coven. Florian had a habit of not doing as he was told, a leftover personality trait from childhood.

"I should have asked Delphine to help me with my lessons," I said, casting a sly glance at my cousin. "She's good at everything, too." In reality, I had no clue whether Delphine was good at flying on a broomstick, but I wasn't one to let facts get in the way of a good setup.

Florian blinked. "Who's Delphine? Another mom from school?"

My face scrunched in annoyance. "Since when do I have

mom friends? No. She's the librarian in town and a member of the coven. How do you not know her?"

Florian shrugged, unperturbed. "It's impossible to know everyone."

"You mean it's impossible to know everyone who doesn't have big boobs and glittery hair."

Understanding flickered in his eyes. "So she's flat-chested and plain. That explains my ignorance."

I folded my arms. "Florian Rose-Muldoon. Wouldn't you like to meet a woman with substance? Delphine is as smart as they come."

Florian looked blank. "And what am I meant to do with a conversationalist?"

I threw up my hands in exasperation. "Delphine is a lovely witch. You should give her a chance."

Florian gave me an odd look. "I'm starting to think maybe *you* want to give her a chance. If she's so wonderful, maybe you should consider changing teams."

I stretched out my hand and wiggled my fingers. "Let's get on with the lesson, please. Otherwise, I might find myself beating you over the head with this broom."

"You wouldn't dare do that to Esmeralda."

I balked. "You named your broomstick Esmeralda?"

"It's much nicer than riding Herbert."

"Who's Herbert?" I queried.

"That was Aster's broomstick. I'm sure he's buried somewhere in her closet. She hasn't ridden for ages. Not since she and Sterling first started dating."

I straddled the broomstick and gripped the leather strap at the end the way I'd done during the broomstick tour.

"What's the deal with Sterling anyway?" I asked. "He's barely around. The only time we ever see him is for Sunday dinner, and I think that's only to escape the wrath of Aunt Hyacinth."

Florian rearranged my hands so that my grip was looser and further apart. "You've noticed, too, have you? I haven't said anything to Aster, but I feel like the whole coven has noticed. He hasn't attended a meeting in months."

"Do you think they're having marital problems?" I asked. It wouldn't surprise me with twin four-year-old boys. He seemed to work nonstop as the president of Hexed Brewing Company, and Aster was the director of several nonprofit organizations, including the tourism board. Their lives had to be exhausting. I only had Marley, who was fairly self-sufficient, and I felt like my life was spiraling out of control half the time.

"I keep meaning to talk to her about it," Florian said. "But I feel like she's been avoiding me lately. We used to spend a lot more time together."

He hopped behind me on the broomstick. I felt it rise gently, as though recognizing his presence.

"For the ones at the broomstick tour, I didn't need to do anything special," I said. "The broomstick seemed to know what to do without any magic from me."

He nodded. "They're especially designed for the tour," Florian said. "For a regular coven broomstick, you need to infuse it with your own magic. Esmeralda obviously has mine, but I'm trying to contain it so that you can take over."

"So what do I do now?" Obviously, I couldn't use a wand, not with two hands gripping the handle and the strap.

"First, you need to focus your will," he said. "That's always rule number one with magic. If you don't focus your will properly, you could end up doing more harm than good."

"Then what?" I asked. "Should I picture us flying?"

"That's part of it," Florian said. "You also need to say the magic word."

"Please?" I joked.

"I thought your magic word was fuggedaboutit."

"Is that Rose-Muldoon humor? If so, you need to work a little magic on that."

"*Scansio*," he said.

I repeated the word. Esmeralda jerked before beginning to climb. "How do I steer her?"

"The same as you would a horse," he said. "Use the leather strap to guide the broomstick. If you want to go higher, pull up. Lower, pull down. You get the idea."

The higher we flew, the more carefree I felt. Strong gusts of wind blew back my hair and I felt empowered. Flying was exhilarating. I didn't know where Marley inherited her fear of heights, but it certainly wasn't from me.

"You're a natural," Florian said. He didn't bother to hide his surprise.

"Inevitably, I was going to be good at something," I yelled over my shoulder. It was difficult to hear with the wind whistling in my ears.

"Too bad broomstick flying isn't as useful as it once was," Florian said.

We flew back and forth over the park and I spotted the gatehouse at the entrance. It was a beautiful structure, with stone walls and powder blue shutters. It reminded me of something from a fairytale.

"Does someone live there?" I inclined my head toward the gatehouse.

"The gatekeeper," Florian said. "An ogre called Finch."

"An ogre?" I echoed.

"That's right. The Finch family has been in charge of the park for decades. His father was the gatekeeper before him, and his grandfather before that."

"You sure like to keep things in the family here," I said. "Didn't we fight the Revolutionary War to avoid all that?"

"Why don't you ask your smart friend Delphine about that? Maybe over a bottle of wine and a topless pillow fight?"

"I don't need to," I said. "I'm taking a local history class at the community college. Maybe I'll learn about it there."

"What made you decide to that? Your schedule already makes me queasy."

"It was after I spoke to that history teacher, Maisie, at the sand sculpture competition," I explained. "She encouraged me to learn more about paranormal history. I thought it would be good for when Marley asked her hundred questions a day. It would be nice to actually know the answer to one of them without telling her to Google it."

"Good thinking," he said. "Maybe I'll join you."

"Join me?" Why on earth would Florian want to do that? He was a lad of leisure.

"There's a new motorcycle I have my eye on," he said. "It's custom designed by Arctic trolls. This might go a long way toward convincing Mother to foot the bill."

I groaned. "Florian, why don't you get a job?"

"I have a job," he argued. "It's called being a Rose-Muldoon. I'm working with the tourism board now. I did so well with the sand sculpture competition that Aster has given me more responsibility. And Mother also has me doing more with the Rose Foundation."

I had to admit, Florian came into his own during the sand sculpture competition. Despite the elf's murder, the competition had been a huge success for the town, which pleased Aunt Hyacinth to no end.

"What about some type of broomstick competition?" I proposed. "Maybe you could have some form of Olympics. This park is perfect for a large crowd."

"Definitely something to consider," he replied. "Speaking of future competitions, how does Marley like her gift from Mother?"

"I assume you mean the unicorn." I hesitated. "Linnea seems to think there are strings attached to Firefly."

"There are always strings attached to Mother's gifts. She uses them as either a carrot or a stick, depending on the situation."

"I don't want Marley to feel obliged to her," I said. "It's an unhealthy dynamic."

He chuckled. "You mean like mine?"

"Now that you mention it, yes."

"Tell Marley to take it and run," Florian suggested. "She's only ten. I imagine Mother is simply trying to win her over while she's still young and impressionable."

That was my aunt's first mistake. Marley was young, but never impressionable.

"Take Esmeralda in for a landing," Florian instructed. "Just ease up on the descent."

Aside from a few bumps, we landed with relative ease.

"Not bad," Florian said. "Next time, we'll practice the hand signals. You need to know them all to pass the test. And you've got to check over your shoulder more. Blind spots are a big deal."

"Hand signals?" I asked. "I need to let go of the broomstick?"

"Only with one hand," he said. "Couldn't you ride a bicycle with one hand?"

I soured. "I never learned to ride a bike."

"Never?" He seemed appalled. "I thought all humans rode bikes. I've seen your movies."

"I didn't do a lot of things, Florian," I said defensively. "My childhood, apparently, wasn't as normal as I thought it was."

Florian dusted off Esmeralda. "Can I ask you something?"

"If it's about the sheriff or Alec Hale, then no."

"No, I don't intrude in romantic affairs like Mother," he said. "I'm wondering why you don't have any mom friends."

Mom friends? "What do you mean?"

"You don't seem to socialize with any of the mothers from Marley's school. I see groups of them out together all the time. Trust me, they're hard to miss. You only spend time with the family socially, unless you count smooching the sheriff or Alec in a bar somewhere."

Although the thought had occurred to me on occasion, I usually brushed it aside. It had been the same in New Jersey, so I didn't expect that part of my life to be much different.

"I'm so busy with work and coven lessons," I said. "When do I have time to hang out with other moms?"

"I think it would be good for you to make an effort," Florian said. "Get together with other women who understand your life."

I laughed. "Trust me, Florian. None of them would understand my life." Paranormal or not, my crazy life would be a foreign concept to them.

"You might be pleasantly surprised," he said.

I examined him closely. "Is this a ploy to meet more women? You're going to use me as a wingman?"

He brightened. "Now that you mention it…No, definitely not. I prefer an unencumbered girlfriend. Honestly, I'm only thinking of you and Marley. She might like it if you were a bit more connected to her world. She's already so entrenched in yours."

Florian was right. Marley was far too invested in my personal life. I needed to find a way to integrate more into hers. "Thanks, Florian. That's actually kinda sweet of you to think of it."

He shrugged those broad shoulders. "I have my moments."

"Maybe your mother was having a sweet moment, too," I said. There was a first time for everything. "Maybe that explains the unicorn."

"Could be," Florian said. "Only time will tell."

CHAPTER 5

"THIS IS AN OUTRAGE. I DEMAND JUSTICE."

Uh oh. Florian and I were barely through the door of Thornhold after my broomstick lesson when we heard Aunt Hyacinth's agitated voice shaking the foundation of the house.

"Thank you, Sheriff. I am well aware you've released him since he's standing right in front of me and I possess the keen power of sight."

Florian and I located my aunt on the phone in her office, dressing down the sheriff. Simon stood in front of the desk, his expression inscrutable.

Aunt Hyacinth acknowledged us with a curt nod as she continued to express her displeasure. "Naturally, he's innocent. He's the household manager for *Thornhold*, not some trailer park mansion in Mystic Town."

Trailer park mansion? Now that I'd love to see.

"If I decide he needs to leave town on an errand, he will leave town," she insisted. "Is that understood?" She paused to listen. "No, of course there are no such errands, but I reserve the right to create one. Good day, Sheriff."

She set the phone on her desk and smiled at us as though she'd just finished a perfectly enjoyable conversation with a dear friend.

"Mother, can we be of assistance?" Florian asked.

Aunt Hyacinth smoothed her white-blond chignon. "No, darling. Thank you for offering. I have the matter well in hand." Her expression hardened when her gaze settled on me. "What good is his infatuation with you if we can't benefit from it?"

I opened my mouth and closed it again. Infatuation seemed a tad strong.

"The sheriff is merely performing his duties," Simon said. "He's treating me as he should. After all, I couldn't expect him to ignore the evidence on my shirt."

Aunt Hyacinth clearly disagreed. "Burn that shirt as soon as it's returned from evidence."

"I can easily remove the stain…" Simon said.

"Absolutely not. That shirt is dead to me now." She adjusted the neckline of her turquoise kaftan. "A starburst martini would be perfection right now, Simon. And bring refreshments for my guests, as well."

"I'm not a guest, Mother," Florian said. "I live here."

"You live below deck," she clarified. "Therefore, you're a guest in the main house."

Simon gave a slight bow and retreated from the office.

Aunt Hyacinth observed us with fresh eagerness. "Have a seat, my lovelies. How was the lesson?"

"She's a natural," Florian said, sitting in the wingback chair opposite her. "Her broomstick license will be no trouble at all."

Aunt Hyacinth flashed a genuine smile. "Finally, an easy task with you. Did you practice turns and hand signals?"

"Next time," Florian said. "I'm confident she'll master those with no problem."

"Excellent." Aunt Hyacinth relaxed. "Simon mentioned you were at the conference, Ember. You're covering it for *Vox Populi*, I assume."

"Yes, Bentley sent me," I said.

"Bentley," she huffed. "I wish Alec would dislodge his head from…" She stopped herself. "My paper needs its editor back. You two are friendly. I don't suppose you've heard from him."

My throat tightened. "No, I haven't. Tanya says he'll be back soon, though."

"He's probably off finishing a novel," my aunt mused. "He's so secretive with his writing. Like an adolescent."

A tray of drinks drifted into the room unescorted and landed on the sideboard. A glass of sweet tea floated to me.

"How did he know?" I asked. Simon never ceased to amaze me.

Florian sipped his wistberry ale. "Mine wasn't difficult to guess."

"Nor mine," Aunt Hyacinth said. "We're creatures of habit."

"Simon is a treasure," I said. "There's no way he had anything to do with the murder."

"Let's hope the suspects the sheriff is about to interview take Simon off the table," Aunt Hyacinth said. She inhaled the aroma of her cocktail before diving in.

I stiffened. "He's going to interview suspects now?"

"That's what he told me," she replied. "He's got three butlers in his office now."

I gulped down the rest of my sweet tea so as not as waste a drop. "I need to go."

"You know where the bathroom is," Florian said. "No need to announce it."

"No, I mean actually go," I said. "To the sheriff's office. I don't want to miss anything."

"Good idea, darling," my aunt said. "Make sure he's conducting a thorough interview. I don't like the idea of Simon being mixed up in any of this mess. Use your feminine wiles."

I opened my mouth to argue about the sexist nature of her comment, but decided silence was the better option.

"I'll do my best," I said, although I couldn't promise anything. As much as the sheriff liked me, he hated my aunt's interference more. I'd have to be careful how I inserted myself into the investigation. Luckily for me, I'd already established a history of meddling on behalf of the paper.

"We'll meet again later this week," Florian said. "Make sure you practice."

I turned to scan the room. "Where's Esmeralda? I'll practice right now."

"You can't fly to the *sheriff's office* without a license," Florian said. "He'll be issuing you a ticket instead of allowing you to sit in on the interview."

Good point. Then I remembered the 'H' rune from Hazel in my pocket. Two birds, one invisibility spell.

"Practice makes perfect, Florian," I said. "Don't worry. I'll bring your broomstick back in one piece. Promise."

Florian eyed me. "It's getting *you* back in one piece I'm more concerned about. I don't want a Humpty Dumpty situation."

I laughed. "I'm not sitting on a wall like an egg-shaped moron."

"No, you'll be much higher," he said. "Even worse."

I placed my empty glass on the tray on my way out. "Then wish me luck."

"May the Goddess of the Moon smile upon you," my aunt said. "But don't get hurt, or I'll consider it a personal insult."

. . .

I took Esmeralda to the patch of lawn at the side of the house and retrieved the rune from my pocket. The only downside to practicing the spell without a witness was that I wouldn't know whether I'd been successful or not. There was also the minor detail of plummeting to my death while invisible. No witnesses for that either.

I rubbed the rune in my palm the way Hazel taught me and focused my will. Essentially, I was attempting to use two spells at once—that involved more magic in one go than I'd ever tried before.

"*Caecus*," I said, and tucked the rune back in my pocket. Then I straddled the broomstick and gripped the leather strap. "Okay, Esmeralda. I'm counting on you not to make a fool of me. We girls need to stick together."

I infused the broomstick with magic like I'd done at the park. I glided into the air with a few jerky movements, then quickly leveled off. The sheriff's office wasn't far, but I needed to figure out where to land without trying to squeeze between buildings. I wasn't advanced enough for parallel broomstick parking.

"Flying is the best," I told the wind. I spotted a long strip of grass not far from the office and circled a few times before I attempted to land. To my relief, no one looked up to see a broomstick flying all by itself. I didn't want to cause panic.

I landed with a thud—not as good as the park landing, but still respectable. I hid Esmeralda in the bushes on the side of the building and proceeded into the sheriff's office.

I walked straight past the reception desk and Deputy Bolan. I thought for sure he'd stop me with his usual scowl.

I found the sheriff at a table in the conference room with three butlers—Belvedere was the only one I recognized. The president of the association seemed the most inconvenienced by the interrogation.

"State your names for the record, please," the sheriff said.

"Theodore Belvedere."

"Joseph Butler." I cocked my head. The butler's name was Butler? Talk about a true calling.

"Jeeves."

"Is that your first name or your last name?" the sheriff asked.

"Both," Jeeves replied.

"Shall I ring a lawyer before we begin?" Belvedere asked.

The sheriff shook his shaggy brown head. "No need for that. I'd just like to have a conversation about your dinner the other night. I understand the three of you were out with the deceased."

"Higgins," Jeeves said. "His name was Higgins."

The sheriff nodded somberly. "Yes, it was. And where did you have dinner?"

"The Flying Pig," Belvedere replied. "We're all staying at the Gryphon, but the food there isn't up to snuff. I've been to the Flying Pig multiple times and have never had a bad meal there."

"So the Flying Pig was your idea?" the sheriff asked.

"That's right," Belvedere said.

"Say, where's Simon?" Joseph Butler asked. "He was at dinner, too."

"I've already spoken to Simon," the sheriff said. "His presence isn't necessary."

"Was the blood on his shirt a match for Higgins?" Belvedere asked.

"That's confidential information," the sheriff replied easily. "Now, tell me about dinner."

"Higgins was out of sorts," Jeeves offered.

"What makes you say that?" the sheriff asked.

"He and I get together for a meal here every year at the conference," Jeeves explained. "This was the first time I've ever seen him inebriated."

"Higgins was drunk?" I asked.

"Yes, Rose," the sheriff said. "That's what inebriated means. I thought you had a good vocabulary." He turned around to address me. "Rose? Where are you?"

Sweet invisible Elvis. No wonder no one bothered me on the way in. I forgot I was still invisible.

"Um, give me one second." How did I reverse the spell on myself? I fished the rune from my pocket and squeezed it in my palm. "*Visus.*"

The sheriff's brow lifted. "You know you shouldn't walk around my office invisible, right? There's an ordinance about that."

"I'm sure there is," I said. "Sorry, it was an accident."

"You were accidentally invisible?" the sheriff queried.

"I once had a master of an estate with a similar problem," Jeeves said. "He'd perform magic whilst drunk and then forget to turn himself visible again. He'd wander the house for days, incensed that no one was paying him any attention." Jeeves chuckled at the memory. "A fine wizard, albeit a tortured one."

"Anyhoo," I said slowly. "I know what inebriated means."

"I know," the sheriff said. "I've seen the evidence firsthand."

I groaned. "Don't make a big deal out of it. I just wanted to confirm that it means the same thing in the paranormal world."

Belvedere smirked. "Yes, my dear. English works exactly the same as a language no matter which tongue speaks it."

I resisted the urge to hex Belvedere with a wart on his nose. It would be harder to resist if I actually knew a spell to achieve that.

"Did Higgins give you any reason as to why he was drinking heavily?" the sheriff asked.

Joseph Butler cast a nervous glance at his companions

before speaking up. "He mentioned a map. I'm pretty sure it was to do with that."

"What kind of map?" I asked. "A map of Starry Hollow?"

"Yes," Jeeves said. "A treasure map to be exact."

The sheriff and I exchanged glances. A treasure map?

"We laughed it off," Belvedere said. "Thought perhaps he was playing a game with us. With his murder, now I'm not so sure."

"What did he plan to do with the map?" the sheriff asked. "Did he intend to search for the treasure?"

Three sets of shoulders shrugged in unison.

"Did he show you the map?" I asked.

"He said he didn't have it on him," Butler said. "Said it was in the small vault in the closet of his hotel room."

"Well, it isn't there now," the sheriff said. "His room has been searched already. Any idea where it might have ended up?"

"Not at all," Belvedere said.

"He did mention a place to me during our dinner conversation," Jeeves said. "It wasn't a direct comment about the map, but he mentioned his intention to visit an inn." He snapped his fingers, trying to remember the name. "It had something to do with ghosts. A well-known inn here in town."

The sheriff slid his palms flat across the table. "Casper's Revenge?"

Casper's Revenge sounded like a rollercoaster.

Jeeves pointed a finger at him. "Yes, that was the name. Apparently, the spirits wait on you, much like a good household manager."

"Thank you, Jeeves," the sheriff said. "That's very helpful."

"Anything else you can think of?" I asked. "Did you see him after dinner?"

"As a matter of fact, I saw Higgins arguing with someone

in the breakfast line before registration," Joseph Butler said. He smacked his forehead. "The new fella. What's his name? Looks mildly Japanese."

"Jenkins," I said. "Trevor Jenkins."

Butler smiled, relieved. "Yes. That's him. I couldn't over-hear them, but Higgins was clearly upset. I'd intended to ask him about it later, but I never got the chance."

Sheriff Nash glanced over his shoulder at me. "You know Jenkins?"

"He's staying at Palmetto House," I said. "I had dinner with him."

"Did you now?" the sheriff asked, his curiosity getting the better of him.

"Along with six others," I said. "Jenkins and Bates are two butlers staying at Linnea's inn."

"I guess it's time to have a chat with Trevor Jenkins, then," the sheriff said. "Gentlemen, that will be all for now. Thank you for your help."

"Can we leave town?" Butler asked. "Not that I have any intention of doing so, of course. I intend to stay for the conference."

"I'd rather you hang around," the sheriff said in a pleasant tone. "Since you'll be here anyway, that doesn't seem like much of an inconvenience."

"It's no problem at all," Jeeves said. "You have my details should you require anything else from me."

"If the household managers can be of any further assistance," Belvedere said, "please don't hesitate to call on us. We live to serve."

The sheriff chuckled. "What a coincidence? So do I."

CHAPTER 6

THE HISTORY of Starry Hollow at the community college was taught by a wereowl called Dr. Gladys Timmons. Dr. Timmons was a short, stout woman with mousy brown hair and large hazel eyes. As she stood in front of the whiteboard, I was seized with the sudden fear that she'd turn her head one hundred eighty degrees. I didn't want to be subjected to an Exorcist moment during my very first lesson.

The bell chimed and Florian slid in beside me. "Good to see you, cousin."

"What are you doing here?" I hissed.

"I told you I was coming."

"I didn't think you'd follow through with it. That's not really your style."

I felt the eyes of the other students on us. An Adonis like Florian wasn't likely to go unnoticed on a college campus.

"Let's get started, shall we?" Dr. Timmons said. "We're here to learn about the history of our town."

"I'm here for credits to graduate," someone grumbled behind us.

"I have no intention of boring you to death, so I will strive to make the class as enjoyable as possible," Dr. Timmons continued. "There will be two major assignments due this term, on top of your regular reading assignments. The first will be a paper on the topic of your choosing. The second will be a group project."

"She doesn't really mean that, does she?" Florian whispered. "That sounds like a lot of work."

I sighed heavily. "Florian, this is school. That's how it works."

"I bet you were really good in school, like Marley."

"Actually, I was an average student," I said. "Nothing like Marley at all."

"Hmm," he said. "Not very Rose-like of you. We tend to excel."

I pressed my foot on top of his. "Be quiet, Florian, if you intend to stay."

Dr. Timmons walked us through the syllabus and told us which reference materials would include the required reading.

I raised my hand.

"What are you doing?" Florian whispered. "Asking questions is a sign of weakness."

I gave him an incredulous look. "Asking questions is a sign of needing an answer."

Dr. Timmons focused her owl eyes on me "Yes?" She scanned the student list. "Your name, please?"

"Ember Rose," I replied. "You have a list of speakers on the syllabus. Are they guest lecturers?"

"Of a sort," Dr. Timmons said. She seemed to notice Florian next to me for the first time. "Hmm. Young man, you have the distinctive look of a Rose."

Florian raked a hand through his telltale hair. "What gave it away?"

"Your pompous air," Dr. Timmons shot back. "Quickly followed by your exquisite physical characteristics."

Florian wasn't sure how to respond. He laughed lightly. "I imagine we appear somewhere in your course."

"Yes," Dr. Timmons said. "That should prove interesting." Her gaze shifted to me. "And you, Miss Rose. You appear to be lacking certain physical traits. Are you a Rose by marriage?"

We burst into laughter.

"Florian, married?" I gasped for breath. "No, I'm his cousin. My father was a Rose. My mother was a Hawthorne."

Dr. Timmons stared at me. "A Hawthorne, you say?"

"That's right," I said. "My mother grew up here. She died not long after I was born, then my father whisked me away to the human world."

"Is that why you do not go by Ember Hawthorne-Rose, in accordance with the custom of your coven?"

"Probably too much of a mouthful for Maple Shade, New Jersey," I replied. I wasn't big on customs, probably why I didn't bother to take my husband's name when we got married, otherwise I would've been Ember Holmes.

Dr. Timmons moved closer to inspect me. "Fascinating." She tweaked my nose. "I thought you were nothing more than a rumor."

I rubbed the edge of my nose. "Nope. Very real."

"And you're taking my class," she said. "Why?"

"Because I want to learn more about paranormal history," I said. "I was raised in the human world. I have zero knowledge, except what I've learned since I've been here."

"It would be helpful for her job, too," Florian said. "She's a reporter for *Vox Populi*."

"Of course," Dr. Timmons said. "Your aunt's enterprise."

"She takes great pride in it," I said. "Sometimes it would

be useful to know more about the town's history when I'm writing a story."

"Absolutely," Dr. Timmons said. "Without a firm grasp of history, we are doomed to repeat it."

Since I had her attention, I decided to dive right in. "Do you know anything about town treasure maps?" I asked.

"I know they'll sell you a replica of one for five silver coins in the local shop." She smiled. "Doubtful you'll find any treasure as a result, though."

"You don't believe in any of the pirate vampire stories?" I asked. I knew all about Captain Blackfang from his son and the owner of the Whitethorn pub, Duncan, otherwise known as Captain Yellowjacket.

"Oh, I know all the stories," Dr. Timmons said. "The treasures themselves I'm not so sure about. They may have existed at one time, but I believe they're long gone. There are far too many ways to unearth treasure using magic."

Just because the treasure didn't exist, didn't mean the murderer knew that. If the killer believed the map would lead to treasure, that was motive enough for the murder of Higgins.

"There will be sufficient time in the semester to discuss local lore," Dr. Timmons said. "Let's at least try to remain on track the first day, eh?"

"Yes, sorry for the thread derail," I said.

"Back to today's lecture," Dr. Timmons said, resuming her place in front of the class. "On the founding of Starry Hollow."

At the end of the lecture, the professor reminded us to choose our paper topics by the end of the week. I already knew I wanted to focus on pirate lore; anything that would assist the investigation.

"I bet Delphine will be a great resource for our papers," I said. "She's incredibly smart and helpful."

"Sounds good to me," Florian said. "If I ace this class, Mother will be sure to bankroll my motorcycle. The Arctic trolls need a good six months' notice to begin work."

I tried not to appear too pleased with myself for slipping Delphine in under his nose. I was a regular Starry Hollow matchmaker. Soon, I'd give Artemis Haverford a run for her money.

"Great," I said, making sure to keep the eagerness out of my voice. "I'll set it up."

Are you sure you want to wear that?

I scrutinized my reflection in the mirror. "What's wrong with it?"

Raoul, my raccoon familiar, came to stand beside me. *You're wearing black from head to toe. It's too depressing. You look like you're ready to go to funeral, or join a convent.*

"Maybe that's the look I'm going for," I said. "I don't want the sheriff to get any ideas."

You invited him to dinner in your home, and you've farmed out your daughter for the evening, Raoul said. *You've already given him ideas.*

Marley was at Florian's, probably enjoying takeout from one of the most expensive restaurants in town. Sometimes it was good to be a Rose.

"It's the result of pure laziness," I said. "I didn't want to get all dressed up to go out and interact with other paranormals. This way, when he leaves, I can climb straight into bed."

He probably thinks before he leaves, he'll climb straight into bed.

"He knows me better than that," I said.

Raoul scampered over to my closet. *What about a red dress? That'll get his attention.*

"I don't need to get his attention," I said. "I'll be the only one here with him."

You've been avoiding red, he said. *Is it because of the vampire?*

Heat rushed to the nape of my neck. "What are you talking about? I'm not avoiding anything because of Alec."

Only because Alec's been avoiding you. Hell's bells, he's been avoiding the whole town. Raoul shook his head in disbelief. *That's some powerful mojo you worked on him.*

"Can we please stop talking about Alec?" I insisted. "Granger will be here soon and I need to cook dinner. I'm behind schedule."

Oh, it's Granger now, is it? He made kissing noises.

"He asked me to call him Granger. Don't be annoying." I paused. "I guess it's too late for that." I adjusted the front of my shirt. "This is what I'm wearing. If he doesn't like it, too bad."

Raoul punched the air. *There's that Jersey girl attitude that gets you in trouble.*

I started to head for the stairs.

Hey, where are you going? he called.

I turned to face him. "Downstairs to make dinner."

Aren't you going to do something with your hair first?

I pressed my lips together and inhaled through my nostrils. "Why, Raoul? What's wrong with my hair?"

Maybe a messy bun, he suggested. *Guys dig that look and you're a natural when it comes to messy.*

"Gee, thanks." I grabbed a hair clip from the dresser and put up my hair. "Messy enough for you?"

Raoul gave me the okay symbol, not so easy for a raccoon.

I hustled downstairs to the kitchen to start dinner.

Are you sure you should be using magic for this? Raoul questioned me. *From what I can tell, you stalled on your magical ABCs. I don't know how smart it is to try and conquer meatloaf.*

"He seems like the comfort food kind of werewolf," I said. "Meatloaf is the logical choice."

Raoul scampered from the countertop and dropped to the floor. *Meatloaf sounds good to me. I'm happy to take the leftovers, I'm just not sure you should be using magic to make it.*

"I realize that we're still getting to know each other," I began, "but I will be the first to tell you that I am a terrible cook. The only thing I'll be putting in front of him without magic is a bowl of macaroni and cheese. And even that comes out of a box. With fake powdered cheese."

Raoul tapped his claw on the floor, thinking. *Maybe you should ask one of your cousins for help.*

"Not Florian," I objected. "He's too spoiled to learn how to cook, even with magic."

That's because he never had to learn, Raoul said. *He always has his mother's staff to tend to his every need. Must be nice.*

"Well, he's not getting waited on right now, not with Simon preoccupied."

I don't know why the sheriff is wasting his time with an investigation, Raoul said. *Everybody knows the butler did it.* He rolled onto his back, unable to contain his glee.

"Hardy har," I said. "I'm glad you're cracking yourself up because no one else is amused."

Raoul flipped back to his paws. *Tough crowd.*

"You need to go so I can concentrate," I said. "Besides, PP3 will wake up soon and he'll freak out if he smells you here." I'd been trying to keep my familiar as far away as possible from my dog. PP3 was set in his ways and adding a new raccoon to the family was not going to go over well.

I'm your familiar, Raoul said. *I should take precedence over a mangy mutt.*

I shook a finger at him. "It's that kind of attitude that makes me not want to introduce you. PP3 is getting on in years and he knows it. I don't want him to think for one second that he's being replaced."

How can he possibly think that? I'm not a pet like him. It's a different relationship.

"We've had enough drastic changes in our lives this year," I said. "I'm surprised he's managed as well as he has."

Oh, look at the time. You'd better get a move on if you expect to finish this before he gets here.

I huffed. Before I could say another word, he leaped onto the counter and disappeared out the kitchen window.

I turned and stared at the magical recipe book. I could rock this meatloaf. I just had to focus. I turned myself invisible and flew on a broomstick without anyone noticing. I should be able to manage a meatloaf.

I held my wand the way Linnea had shown me and focused my will. I pictured a juicy meatloaf cooking in the oven. I felt my eyes sting from the onion and imagined Worcestershire sauce. I infused the meat with tenderness, not the emotional kind, of course. I meant for the meat. Once I was certain all the elements were in place, I said in a firm voice, *"Coquino."*

I waited a minute before opening the oven door, afraid to see the results. I tried to peer in the window, but it was too dark to see the interior of the oven. What was the spell for creating light? It made me nervous to try to do too many spells at once. I'd already done it once today and I knew how magic depleted a body's resources. I didn't want magic to drain my energy before the sheriff arrived. I had to build up to it like my more powerful cousins. I glanced at the clock on the wall. I didn't have much time left. I aimed my wand and said, *"Lumina."*

Every light in the cottage flickered and died.

"Oh, no!" What had I done? Sheriff Nash would be here any minute.

I touched the oven door and it felt warm. Without light, I wouldn't be able to see whether the meatloaf was done. Not that it mattered. We couldn't have dinner like this. Then I made my next mistake.

I opened the oven door.

Ground beef exploded. Bits of meat flew in every direction, sticking to my hair and clothes. A tiny piece of onion smacked me in the eye.

"It burns!" I ran to the sink to rinse out the onion and soothe my eyeball. I glanced at my reflection in the microwave door. My eye was bright red and angry-looking. Chunks of meat hung from my hair. This was a complete disaster. Raoul was right. I should have known better.

PP3 appeared at my feet, barking.

I placed a hand on my hip. "What? Like I did this on purpose. I need to run upstairs before he gets here, or I'll never hear the end of it."

No sooner did the words leave my mouth than the doorbell rang. I closed my eyes and tried to steady my breathing. This was a bad omen. I should never have invited him to dinner. This was the gods' punishment for what I did to Alec. The universe was telling me, in no uncertain terms, that it disapproved of me.

PP3 ran circles around my legs, yapping up a storm. I scooped him up in my arms and he began licking the ground beef from my shoulder.

"That's enough," I said. "You need to behave for our guest. I have a feeling he won't be staying very long."

PP3 squirmed in my arms. I placed him gently on the kitchen floor and closed the door behind me. I squared my shoulders and raised my chin a fraction before heading to the door.

When I finally opened the door, the sheriff had just raised

his arm to ring the bell again. He took one look at me and burst into laughter.

"Wow," was all he could manage.

I pretended there was nothing amiss and simply held open the door. "Come in, Sheriff."

"I told you to call me Granger, especially when I'm coming over to your house for dinner." He crossed the threshold and immediately noticed the lack of light. It became even more noticeable once I closed the front door, as we were suddenly bathed in darkness.

I heard the Sheriff's low chuckle. "No light, and you've drenched yourself in meat. You're really trying to set the mood, aren't you, Rose? I would've thought you'd want to take things a bit slower."

"Trust me, this was not what I had in mind when I started."

"No doubt. What can I do to help?" Although it was dark, I could feel his presence. I could also hear PP3 scratching at the kitchen door.

"I'm sorry," I said. "I tried to make you a nice dinner. That clearly didn't happen."

"What about the lights? Did you blow a fuse or some-thing?" He edged closer to me. "I know how your temper tends to flare."

"Ha ha. I don't know," I said. "I tried to add light to the oven so I could check on the meatloaf. Instead, all the lights went out. Too much magic in one day for this witch."

Even in the darkness, I could feel the Sheriff's grin. "You're making meatloaf for me?"

"It seemed up your alley," I said.

He sniffed the air. "Yep. Smells good. Mind if I have a taste?" Before I could respond, I felt his warm hand on my shoulder.

"You may as well," I said. "It's either this, or peanut butter and jelly."

I felt his lips on the curve of my neck and shuddered as he nibbled my bare skin.

"I do like peanut butter," he murmured. "But this tastes good, too."

"Are you actually getting any meat?" I asked. It was difficult to talk when he was having such a mind-numbing effect on me.

"I'm working on it," he said. "Might take a while. Hope you don't mind."

Did I mind? "I told you I want to take things slow." I forced out the words, despite my body's inclination to go faster.

"Why do you think I'm still on your neck?" he teased. I heard the desire in his voice and my whole body tingled in response.

"You should probably stop," I said unconvincingly.

"I brought you a present," he said between nibbles. "Maybe you can try it on now. See if it fits."

"I'm not trying anything on while I'm covered in meat," I said.

"You could try me on," he said suggestively. "See if I fit."

Sweet baby Elvis. I was going to be a puddle on the floor if he kept this up much longer.

A sharp bark from PP3 brought me to my senses. I snapped back and cleared my head.

"We should really fix these lights," I said in a no-nonsense voice. "Let me see what I can do."

"I'll help you," he said. "I'm pretty good with my hands."

I moaned and stepped out of his reach.

"I need to go into the kitchen where the dog is," I said. "You know he's not sure about you yet." PP3 was territorial. He didn't like the smell of the wolf. "I need my wand."

"Or we could go out to eat," he suggested. "Might be easier."

I hesitated. I needed to clean myself up either way, and, after what just happened between us, it was probably safer to pass the evening outside of the cottage.

"All right then, Granger," I said. "Let me run upstairs and clean myself up." It wasn't worth using magic at this point. I didn't trust myself.

"Take your present," he said. "Maybe you'll decide to wear it." He thrust a gift bag into my hand.

I fumbled toward the steps, clutching the bag, and managed to trip on my way up. There was no way to disguise the loud thump.

"You need a hand, Rose?" he asked. "I'd be happy to escort you to your room."

"No, no," I called in a panic. "Don't come up. I'll be fine."

In the still of the darkness, I heard him chuckle again.

"Wereass," I hissed.

And the chuckle quickly escalated to a belly laugh.

CHAPTER 7

THE GIFT from the sheriff was a red T-shirt that read *Proud Broomstick Mama*. He'd accused me of being the paranormal version of a helicopter mom recently, so the gift was intended to be funny.

"You're actually going to wear it?" he said, as we left the cottage.

"I'm proud, remember? Says so right here." I pointed to my chest.

"I like you in red," he said. "I also like when you draw attention to your chest."

I rolled my eyes. He was no better than Florian. "Thanks for the shirt. It's cute."

"Where would you like to go to dinner?" he asked. "Somewhere new? Or a trusted favorite like the Lighthouse?"

"How about we try the Flying Pig?" I suggested.

He broke into a grin. "Rose, you have a detective's brain. Has anyone ever told you that?"

"I prefer to have my own brain, thanks." I stopped in the driveway. "Don't you think I should drive? After all, I invited you to dinner."

He didn't hesitate. "No, thanks, Rose. I've seen the way you drive. Must be those New Jersey highways. Adds an extra ten pounds to your pedal foot."

I slipped into the passenger seat of his car without complaint. He could withstand much more alcohol than I could and still drive in a sober state. If the latter half of the night went anything like the former half, I was going to need a copious amount of alcohol to power through.

The Flying Pig was located off Coastline Drive, not far from the Whitethorn. It wasn't as old or atmospheric as the ancient pub, but it had its own appeal. The wooden sign creaked as it swung in the sea breeze and the image of a winged pig seemed to glow in the moonlight.

"Have you ever been here?" I asked, standing out front to take in the view. The stars twinkled above and I listened to the gentle lapping of the waves on the rocks below.

"Not often," the sheriff said. "No particular reason, though. I just have my usual watering holes, I guess."

"I trust the butlers' judgment," I said. "If the food and service is good enough for them, it has to be above average."

"I'll take that leap of faith," he replied.

The moment we stepped inside, I knew we'd made a mistake.

"Alec." I couldn't disguise the shock in my voice. He looked amazingly good, probably because I hadn't seen him in weeks. He was back to wearing custom suits and slicked-back hair. His green eyes glinted in the dim artificial light.

"Good evening, Hale," the sheriff said stiffly.

The vampire inclined his head in that civil manner he'd mastered so well. "Sheriff. Miss Rose."

Miss Rose. I tried not to react to his formal address. When he was under the opposite spell, he'd called me Ember and I'd relished the change.

"When did you get home?" I asked. I made sure to cloak

my thoughts because Alec had a habit of reading them; one of the perks of being a powerful vampire.

"Last evening," he replied. His intelligent gaze shifted to Sheriff Nash. "Date night?"

"It is, as a matter of fact." I heard the note of pride in the sheriff's voice. Ugh. "Last time I saw you was on stage doing your best impression of 'the Boss.'"

Alec's placid expression remained intact. "Ah, yes. Springsteen. I do believe I outperformed you that evening, Sheriff." His gaze lingered on me. "In every respect."

My cheeks were on fire. I knew exactly what he was implying and I hoped the sheriff didn't glean anything from it. It seemed Alec's desire to one-up the sheriff took precedence over his desire to block out the events of that night.

Before I had a chance to change the subject, a lively woman came bounding over to us like a busty Saint Bernard.

"This place is so quaint, Alec," she cooed. "I adore it."

My whole body tensed as her palms stroked his chest. "Who's your friend?" I asked, desperately hoping to keep a neutral tone.

"Miss Rose. Sheriff Nash. I'd like you to meet Holly." He looked down at his companion. "Miss Rose works for me at the newspaper."

Holly's mouth formed a tiny 'o.' "How exciting! A girl reporter."

Seriously? What century were we in?

"I prefer the term 'investigative journalist,'" I said. Beside me, the sheriff snickered.

"Old friends, Hale?" Sheriff Nash queried.

Alec opened his mouth to speak, but Holly jumped in first. "I feel like I've known him forever, but we only met recently in Rainbow's End."

"I didn't realize you went to the West Coast," I said. I thought he was somewhere in the New York area, not that it mattered. He was far away from me, and that was the point.

"It was sufficiently far," he said vaguely.

Bingo.

"And you've come for a visit already, Holly?" I asked. "Seems quick."

Holly's laugh was piercing. "I know, right? If I like it, I just might stay." She rubbed Alec's chiseled cheek, and I fought the urge to smack her hand away. Sheriff Nash may have been the werewolf among us, but I was fighting a severe case of animal instinct.

"Your table is ready, Mr. Hale," the host said.

Thank the gods.

When the host returned, I adopted my friendliest tone. "Would you mind seating us as far away from your last guests as possible? He's my boss and I feel awkward sitting too close to him when he's on a date."

The host turned to look at where he'd seated Alec and Holly. "Of course, miss. Not to worry." He steered us to a booth at the opposite end of the restaurant.

"I don't picture Alec with a nymph like Holly," the sheriff said nonchalantly, as he opened his menu.

"She's a nymph?" I asked.

"That's what she smelled like," he said.

I wrinkled my nose. "How does a nymph smell?"

"With her nose," he shot back and pounded his fists in the table like it was a drum.

I groaned. "Does she smell like the sea or something?"

"She would if she were a water nymph. A naiad. But Holly's a hamadryad. She smells like the forest."

I leaned back and regarded him carefully. "And that appeals to you, I guess? As a werewolf?"

He shrugged. "The smell does." He cast a curious look in Holly's direction. "Not so much the nymph herself."

Her laugh pierced the air again, making me cringe. It was worse than nails on a chalkboard. I couldn't imagine how Alec's enhanced vampire hearing was tolerating the sound when my average ears were in agony. She banged her hands on the table, shrieking at something Alec said.

"Okay, he's not *that* funny," I grumbled. His humor was too dry to warrant hysterical laughter.

"You know, you and I could talk, instead of watching them," the sheriff said. "If I recall correctly, we're on our own date."

I focused on the menu. "Let's decide what to eat, and then we'll decide what to ask the staff about the night Higgins was here."

"I see." The sheriff closed his menu. "Back to business, eh, Rose?"

"You know what you want already?" I asked, studying the list of specials. Everything sounded delicious.

"Always do," he said cryptically. "You seem a little uncertain, though."

"Can you blame me?" I asked. "There are several good options here."

"Not to me."

I tapped the menu. "There are a couple dishes where I like the mains but not the sides, or vice versa. Maybe they'll let me mix it up."

"I guess that's where we differ, Rose. I only see one good option and it's perfect exactly the way it is."

I finally settled on braised pork with a side of root vegetables. The description included herbs and spices I'd never heard of and I was eager to try them. We ordered from an energetic server named Mikey with the telltale ears of an elf.

"You never said whether the blood on Simon's shirt belonged to Higgins," I said.

"That's because you know it did, Rose," he replied.

"But you don't think Simon had anything to do with it, do you?" There was no way Simon would kill anyone, and certainly not with a corkscrew.

"My guts says no," the sheriff said. "But there were no prints on the corkscrew, and no blood on anyone else."

"So someone was smart enough to wipe down the weapon, but not smart enough to take it with them when they fled?"

"Or they didn't wipe it down and fled when they realized what they'd done, leaving the weapon behind."

I tapped my fork on the table. "Ghost prints?"

"Or gloves," he said. "Half those butlers wear them."

I immediately thought of Bates and his white gloves. "If there were gloves involved, there would definitely be traces of blood on them."

"If the killer wore gloves, they could have disposed of them anywhere," the sheriff said.

"Hey, Mikey," I said, once the elf delivered our drinks. "Were you working here the other night when a group of butlers came in? They're hard to miss since they dress like a formal boy band. I'm surprised they don't walk in V formation. They're here for a conference."

Mikey's head bobbed up and down enthusiastically. "One of the best tables I ever waited on. I had to stop them from going behind the bar to pour their own drinks when we got slammed." He tittered. "One of them offered to iron the tablecloth because it had a crease in the wrong place."

"They wouldn't know where to start in my house," I said. No wonder Simon never came inside. He likely suspected he'd be driven to dip into Aunt Hyacinth's smelling salts.

"Send him over to the cottage now because he won't see a thing," the sheriff teased.

"I actually texted Florian to see if he can magic the lights back on while we're here," I said smugly. "Marley needs to go to bed anyway."

Mikey glanced from the sheriff to me. "Did you have a question about the butlers, or did you just want to confirm they were here?"

The sheriff cleared his throat. "Yes, of course. Did you happen to overhear any of their conversation?"

"Bits and pieces," Mikey said. "One of them was hammered by the end of the meal. He babbled to the others about a map." He scratched the back of his neck. "Sounded like his boss just died or something, too. He was stressed. The dude had a lot going on."

"Did you notice any disagreements or anything unusual?" the sheriff asked.

"No, they were all very polite, even the drunk one." Mikey perked up. "Plus, I got a huge tip." He hesitated. "That I will absolutely report on my taxes."

Sheriff Nash gave him a comforting smile. "No worries, Mikey. I'm not the tax police."

The butlers' account of the evening seemed to jive with Mikey's recollection. That was reassuring.

"Do you remember how many there were?" the sheriff asked.

Mikey tugged on the point of his ear. "Five, I think. I can check the merchant copy of the tab." He gave the sheriff a pointed look. "I assume this is official business."

"Absolutely. You'd be serving your community with more than food for a change, Mikey," the sheriff said.

The elf beamed like Santa was leaving him in charge of the North Pole on Christmas. "Let me check on your food and I'll be back with a copy." He saluted the sheriff and I stifled a laugh.

"How's your cocktail, Rose?" he asked, his attention back on me.

I smacked my lips together. "Tastes like a rum and Coke." I'd ordered something called a Tall Stranger. It was served in a Pilsner-style glass and looked thick and syrupy, just the way I imagined it.

"I don't know what Coke is, but you're probably right about the rum." The sheriff flashed a lopsided grin. "I don't suppose you'll let me have a sip."

"Sure, I will," I replied. "Right after the pig on the sign out front takes flight."

The werewolf's dark eyes glittered like two onyx. "You've got some funny hang-ups, Rose."

"I'm not a werewolf," I said. "I don't think that means my preferences should be categorized as hang-ups."

"Werewolves aren't the only kind to share food and drinks," he said. "Besides, it's not like we run around stealing food off plates and sipping drinks willy nilly."

"Oh no?" I said. "I've eaten with Wyatt, don't forget."

The sheriff snorted. "Yeah, well, my brother is his own wolf. Nobody would argue with that. Some of us reserve our sharing for more…special cases."

I squinted at him. "Are you trying to tell me that you and Bolan don't suck the opposite ends of spaghetti together?" The image of them nudging meatballs to each other with their noses nearly had me in stitches.

"Is that a New Jersey reference, Rose?"

"*Lady and the Tramp*," I said. "I thought Disney transcended realms."

"Nope, sorry." He fiddled with his empty glass. "How would you like to get to know more about the pack?"

"I'm taking a class at the community college on local history. Maybe there'll be a section on the werewolves of Starry Hollow."

He tapped the rim with such force that the glass wobbled.

"I'm not talking about our history, although you'd likely learn a good deal."

I eyed him closely. "Sheriff, you seem nervous."

"Granger," he insisted. "We're on a date, Rose." He cleared his throat again. Yep. Definitely nervous.

"Fine. Granger, you seem nervous. What's up?" I flashed a cheesy smile. "Is that better?"

"The Nash family is hosting a pack barbecue and I was wondering if you'd like to join me."

I choked on my mouthful of thick syrup. "You want me to meet your family?" For the love of Abraham Lincoln, we said we'd take it slow. How did a family barbecue fit in?

He shifted uncomfortably in his seat. "You already know Wyatt, and my mama's been pestering me..." He trailed off.

"Your *mother* wants to meet me? Why?" I had no experience with mothers. Zero. My mother died when I was an infant, and Karl's mother disowned him when we told them about my pregnancy. I never met my grandmothers. Aunt Hyacinth was the closest to a mother figure I had and that was saying something.

"She's my mother. Naturally, she's interested in my life," Sheriff Nash said.

"You mean she meddles," I replied.

"She really doesn't." He gave me a hard look. "Do you think Wyatt would be half as bad as he is if my mother chose to meddle? She gave up boxing his ears years ago."

Maybe she should've kept at it, for the good of the female gender. "I don't know if we're at the meet-the-parents stage of this relationship," I said.

"I'll take good care of you, Rose," he said. "Besides, it's an all-day party, not an inquisition. My cousin's band is playing. Lots of good food. It'll be fun."

"Will it just be werewolves?"

"Mostly, but there are some mixed partnerships. My

cousin Vinnie is married to a werebear. He always liked 'em big."

"Will I be the only witch?" I asked.

He raised his glass to get Mikey's attention. "Not sure. Does it matter?"

"I guess not."

"It'll be a chance for you to meet paranormals outside of your aunt's influence," the sheriff said.

"I thought no one was outside of her sphere of influence," I said, smiling.

"The pack is pretty strong," he replied. "We stand up to the Rose-Muldoons when it counts."

I frowned. "It sounds like I may not be a popular choice."

He reached across the table and squeezed my hand. "You're my choice. Doesn't matter whether it's a popular one. For what it's worth, everybody liked Linnea. They were mighty disappointed in Wyatt when he screwed that up."

I nodded. "We're all on the same page there."

"No pressure," he said. "If you don't like the idea, I'll drop it."

Before I could respond, Mikey returned to the table with our food. "I also brought the merchant tab." He set a copy on the table. "If you have any more questions, I'll do what I can to help."

"Thanks, Mikey," the sheriff said. "Appreciate it."

A peal of laughter rang out, which quickly evolved into a loud snort. I groaned. "Aren't they on dessert yet?"

"Relax, Rose. They're having fun." He glanced over his shoulder. "Well, *she* is. Hard to tell with Hale. He always looks like someone's stolen his favorite toy."

I swallowed hard. Maybe because someone had.

"Okay, Granger," I said, surprising myself. If Alec was willing to find other ways to entertain himself, then so was I. "I like to eat and listen to music. I'll come to your barbecue."

He visibly relaxed. "That's great, Rose. It'll be a good time. You won't regret it."

I offered a threatening smile. "Just don't try to share my food, or you'll end up in a body cast."

He held up his hands. "Consider me warned."

CHAPTER 8

ON THE WAY to the convention center the next morning, I stopped by the sheriff's office to check with Deputy Bolan on any updates. He made every effort to ignore me until I planted myself between him and the coffee machine.

"I'm heading over to the conference now," I said. "It would be helpful to know if there's been new information before I stick my foot in my mouth."

He gave my shoes a withered look. "And here I thought you liked the taste of cheap pleather."

I placed a hand on my hip. "Listen, Martian Man."

"There are rules about disparaging law enforcement. You would know that if you paid attention to rules other than those of your own creation."

Before I could answer, the deputy took the opportunity to dart around me and swiped the coffee pot from its base.

"A simple yes or no, Bolan," I said. "Any updates?"

"Didn't you discuss the case last night on your *date*?" the deputy sneered.

"I know you're happily married to the best husband in the

world," I began, "but you give the distinct impression that you have a thing for your boss."

"That makes two of us," he shot back.

Ooh. Touché, leprechaun.

"What's going on? What's happened?" A middle-aged woman rushed into the office, her cheeks flushed and her loose chignon sliding down to the nape of her neck. Her spider-like body teetered on a pair of skinny heels. She smelled like she'd bathed in an English garden on the way over. Better than a garbage dump, I supposed.

"Calm down, ma'am," Deputy Bolan said. He moved in front of her to slow her frenetic pace. "How can we help?"

"Higgins," she said breathlessly. "My butler is here for a conference. I received a troubling call…"

Her butler? I thought Higgins' estate had lost its owner recently.

Deputy Bolan's expression clouded over. "I see. May I have your name?"

"Laura Stanhope." She sucked in air. "Please tell me nothing is amiss." She moaned. "Oh, don't be a fool, Laura. Of course, something is amiss. They've summoned you to the sheriff's office. Is he in trouble for something? Whatever the issue is, I can promise you it wasn't him. Higgins is as trustworthy as they come. My mother's judgment was impeccable."

Deputy Bolan and I exchanged bemused glances. We weren't often on the same page, but I clearly saw 'nut job' etched in the lift of his greenish eyebrows.

"Come this way, Mrs. Stanhope," he said, guiding her to the conference room.

"*Miss* Stanhope," she corrected him fiercely.

"My apologies, Miss Stanhope," he said. "Sheriff Nash will be in to speak with you in a moment."

"Thank you."

We heard her muttering to herself as she disappeared into the interrogation room.

"Why don't you babysit her while I get the sheriff?" Deputy Bolan asked.

"Really? You trust me to do that?"

"It'll only be two minutes," he replied. "How much harm can you do?" He paused. "On second thought, I'll sit with Miss Stanhope. You fetch the sheriff."

"Deal." I hurried to his office. I didn't want to miss a second of Miss Stanhope. Not when we might finally get a break in the case.

"What's the matter, Rose?" Sheriff Nash looked up from his desk to see me framed in the doorway.

"I'm a complete witch."

"This is news?" he queried.

"I don't mean the magical kind," I said. Laura Stanhope was near hysteria and the only thing I could think of was that she could represent a break in the case. Where was my humanity?

"What'd you do now? Break the copy machine with pictures of your butt? Don't sweat it. We have pixies on call that can fix it in a jiffy."

"Nothing like that." I pushed down the shame and continued. "You have someone in the interrogation room. Laura Stanhope."

"That was quick," he said. "I didn't expect her until tomorrow."

"She seems like she came in a hurry," I said. "You'd better bring a box of tissues." And a straightjacket.

He grabbed a box from the shelf behind his desk. "Thanks for the tip. You sitting in?"

"If you don't mind."

"If I minded, I wouldn't offer." He strode past me. "You smell nice, Rose. That a new perfume?"

"No, I was in the woods with PP3 before I got here and I fell in a bramble patch. I didn't have time to shower."

He shook his head. "Only you, Rose."

It had been quite the predicament. PP3 had run circles around the bramble patch, barking at it like it had ensnared me. I had to calm the dog before I could extricate myself from its grasp without slicing my arm to bits. It occurred to me afterward that I should have tried to use magic, but, after a string of recent fiascos, I wasn't too eager to try a new spell.

Laura Stanhope was muttering under her breath when we arrived. She had a glass of water in front of her and was in the process of retrieving a vial of swirling purple potion from her handbag.

"What's in the vial?" Deputy Bolan asked, as she moved to pop off the lid.

"Mommy called it my morning vitamin," she said. "It's a rather strong anti-anxiety potion. It calms me down. I'm prone to anxiety, you see. Always have been. Mommy said I was born screaming and never stopped. Said I drove Daddy to an early grave."

Great balls of dysfunction. One more reason to be thankful for my relationship with Marley.

The sheriff approached the table. "Any chance you could hold off on drinking the potion until we've had a conversation? I'd prefer you to be lucid."

"Oh, I'll be lucid," she said, "It takes the edge off. I know you have bad news. I saw it in my tea leaves this morning."

Under normal circumstances, I would've scoffed at the claim, but living in Starry Hollow changed my perspective on that sort of thing.

Sheriff Nash pulled out a chair and sat across from Laura. "I'm afraid you're right, Miss Stanhope. It appears Higgins was murdered at the PEMA conference."

Her face crumpled. "Higgins is dead? Murdered?" she whispered. "How? Why? By whom?"

The shameful part of me was disappointed by her mild reaction. I was anticipating torturous wails and a beating of the chest. Maybe a sobbing drop to the knees. At the very least, a *Real Housewives* table flip. This was far too reasonable.

"That's what we're trying to piece together," the sheriff said. "We've spoken to a few butlers he spent time with before he died, and a couple of them mentioned a map. Do you know anything about that?"

Laura's nose wrinkled. "A map? Why the gods would a map be significant? He got lost in town and was killed in the course of a robbery?"

"Not exactly." The sheriff watched her attentively. "More like a treasure map."

"Oh." Her expression passed from confused to enlightened. "He spoke about the treasure map?"

"You know about it?" the sheriff asked.

"Of course I know about it," she said. "It's been sitting in my mother's vault for years, ever since my grandfather died and she inherited it."

"Apparently, it's not in your mother's vault anymore," the sheriff said. "Higgins seems to have brought it with him to Starry Hollow and now it's missing."

Laura fell silent, processing the information.

"Miss Stanhope," Deputy Bolan said gently, "do you have any idea why he would do that?"

"Take the map?" She seemed confused by the question. "How should I know?"

"Has he ever stolen from your family before?" I asked.

Laura fixed me with a venomous stare. "How dare you. Higgins would *never* steal from us."

"Then how do you explain the map?" the sheriff asked. "Did he have permission to take it?"

Laura fidgeted with her vial. "Whatever the reason, it wouldn't have been to steal. Higgins was loyal to the estate *and* the family."

"So you gave your permission for him to take it?" the sheriff prodded.

"No, but since the map belongs to me now, I grant him permission posthumously," Laura said.

The sheriff slumped against his chair. "The law doesn't work that way, Miss Stanhope."

"The law works whatever way I choose," she snapped. "I'm a Stanhope, for Mother Nature's sake."

Whoa. That was the kind of pompous statement that was sure to set the sheriff's teeth on edge.

"Have you ever seen the map?" I interjected, before the sheriff could express his irritation. "Would you be able to tell us anything about it?"

She pulled a tissue from the box on the table and dabbed the corners of her eyes, careful not to smear her mascara. "As a matter of fact, I can. I saw it recently."

"What was the occasion?" Deputy Bolan asked.

Laura popped the lid off and downed the potion before anyone could object. "We reviewed the contents of the vault with the family lawyer after Mommy died."

"We?" the sheriff asked. "You have any siblings?"

"No, thank the gods," Laura said. "I'd make a terrible sister. I don't like to share, you see." She cringed as though 'share' was a dirty word. "We, as in Higgins, the lawyer, and me."

"What's the lawyer's name?" Deputy Bolan asked, taking notes.

"Stu Storey." She plucked a business card from her handbag. "Here's his information. He's been with our family for generations. Vampires make the best lawyers. If you're ever in the market, the undead are the way to go."

"Thanks for the tip," the sheriff said. "When you went through the vault, did you notice anything strange about Higgins? Did he react to the sight of the map?"

Laura appeared thoughtful. "He was interested from the point of view of someone who likes tall tales. Higgins was an avid reader. In fact, his favorite author is a local resident. Alec Hale. Maybe you've heard of him?"

The sheriff didn't miss a beat. "Yes, we know Alec Hale."

I refrained from mentioning that he was my boss. I didn't want to be pestered for a signed copy of his book, not from someone as unstable as Laura seemed.

"Were you interested in the map?" I asked.

Laura laughed. "I'm not interested in treasure, if that's what you're asking. My family has more money than it knows what to do with. I don't think we could be poor if we tried."

"Do you know the origin of the map?" the sheriff asked. "How it came into your family's possession?"

"I'm afraid not," she said. "All I can tell you are some of the locations specified on the map."

The sheriff leaned forward. "Well, that would definitely help."

I knew what he was thinking. If the murderer had the map and was hunting for the treasure at any of the locations, we might track him down before he found it.

Laura gave him a demure smile. "Glad to help, Sheriff." She snapped her fingers at Deputy Bolan. "Little man, if you can find me a regular map of the town, I can point to the places I remember. I have a visual memory."

The leprechaun bristled. "The name is Deputy Bolan. Ember, would you be so kind as to bring us a map?"

I peered at him. "You know I don't work for you, right?"

He rolled his eyes as he hopped off the chair. "Be right back."

"Maybe you could manifest a map," the sheriff said to me. "All that training you're doing might prove useful at some point."

Laura gazed at me with renewed interest. "Oh, a witch?"

"That's right," I said, injecting a note of pride into my voice. "Ember Rose, direct descendant of the One True Witch."

Laura blinked. "How sweet. I'm afraid I don't know very much about witches. I'm descended from a long line of norns on my mother's side."

The sheriff covered his laugh with a loud cough. "The Rose family is very prominent here in Starry Hollow, Miss Stanhope. In fact, their butler had dinner with Higgins the night before he died."

"Is that so?" Laura asked.

"What's a norn?" I inquired.

Laura tucked a loose strand of hair behind her ear. "Norns were once magical beings, but many of us ceased the practice of magic generations ago."

"For a reason?" I asked.

"Not really. Each generation passed down less and less information, until there was no knowledge left to impart."

That seemed a great loss. Maybe it was because the discovery of magic was still new to me, but I couldn't imagine letting something so incredible fall by the wayside.

"Do you know Trevor Jenkins?" I asked.

Her surprise was evident. "Of course. Jenkins serves the estate where my uncle lives. Mommy and Uncle Larry weren't very close, so I don't know Jenkins, although my uncle did attend the funeral."

"Would Jenkins know about the map?" I asked.

"I should think so," Laura said. "It was one of the reasons for Mommy and Uncle Larry's falling out. Grandpapa left the map to Mommy when he died and she refused to give it to Uncle Larry."

I could tell from the sheriff's body language that we were having the same thought. Jenkins was already on our interrogation list. Good thing I was already planning to track him down at the conference to ask him about the argument with Higgins the morning of the murder.

Deputy Bolan reappeared with a town map. "Here you go." He placed it open in front of Laura.

"I recognize a few spots," she said, retrieving a pen from her bottomless handbag. She began marking places with an X. "I didn't study the map closely, mind you, so it may not be completely accurate. I do remember the original map had a symbol of two crossed daggers dripping with blood." She shivered. "I don't do well with blood."

"Whatever you can remember is fine," the sheriff said. "It's not like you expected to be quizzed on it."

"Certainly not," Laura replied, dropping the pen back into her bag. "But I want to do whatever I can to help you find his killer. In fact, I've decided to stay right here in town at the Aphrodite Hotel until you apprehend the guilty party. Higgins was like family to me and I've only recently lost Mommy. He *must* be avenged."

"We can't promise vengeance," the sheriff said. "But we can promise justice."

She snapped her handbag closed. "I'll take it."

After the conversation with Laura, I headed back to the convention center for the continuation of the conference. I needed to follow up with Jenkins on the alleged argument with Higgins at breakfast the morning of the murder. The Sheriff and I agreed that I would have the initial conversation with Jenkins since I'd already established a relationship with him. We figured he'd be more likely to speak freely without the sheriff present.

With the conference in full swing, I hunted him down in the room labeled 'Master Bedroom.' A small group was assembled in the room, listening to a lecture on bedroom etiquette. I had no idea how much thought went into their duties. They discussed everything from hospital corners to tact when the owner of the house had an unexpected overnight guest. They were the epitome of discretion. Once again, I found myself wondering about Simon's role at Thornhold. No doubt the man knew where all the bodies were buried. The brightly colored kaftans with fluffy animal heads fooled no one. Aunt Hyacinth was a force to be reckoned with.

I spotted Jenkins at the back of the room. He seemed more interested in the diamond-encrusted candlesticks than the lecture. When he saw me watching him, he straightened and returned his focus to the lecturer.

As I started toward him, the lecturer noticed my presence. "Ah, you're the reporter. Have you come to cover my lecture? I'd be happy to provide you with the notes afterward."

"Yes," I enthused. "That would be great, thank you." I winked at Jenkins, who suppressed a smile.

"No photographer?" the lecturer complained. "Last year, I was featured on the front page."

Hmm. Slow news day, then.

I pulled my phone from my pocket and snapped his picture.

"That isn't my best side," he objected.

"Don't worry. I'm a witch," I said. "I'll work my magic on it." That got a few snickers in the crowd.

The lecturer continued with his commentary. "Thankfully, the days of chamber pots are long over."

"Too right!" someone called from the back. "Butlers today don't know how easy they have it."

"In my day, we didn't have kitchens attached to the main residence," someone else said. "I had a staff of pixies that flew the food in through the windows. Made it terribly drafty during meals."

How old were these butlers? After a few minutes of listening to their anecdotes, I realized that Jenkins had moved beside me.

"You look as bored as I feel," I whispered. "Are you starting to regret your first conference?"

"I'd be lying if I said no," Jenkins replied. "To be fair, I think I would find any conference dull. I'm not one for lectures."

"Then you would hate my history class," I said. "It's one hundred percent lectures. And we don't get to stand in a pretty room like this to do it, either."

"Regretting your choice to become educated?" he queried. Amusement danced in his dark eyes.

"Actually, the class itself is interesting," I said. "I'm new to the paranormal world, so everything is still shiny and new to me."

When the lecturer began to drone on about the right way to restock bathroom supplies, that was my cue to leave.

"How about a coffee to stay awake for the rest of the sessions?" I asked. "I saw a coffee kiosk in the lobby area."

Jenkins nodded mutely and followed me out the door with the stealth I'd expect from a vampire.

"A plain latte with a shot of success, please," I said.

The kiosk was manned by a troll whose fingers were so huge, I watched to see whether he could operate the machinery without breaking anything.

Jenkins smiled. "Success, yes. I'll have the same, please."

I looked at him askance. "What kind of success are you

looking for? Top marks as the new household manager? That's unlikely if you keep ditching lectures."

"I could ask you the same question," he said. "What kind of success are you looking for? Finishing the story in time to meet your deadline?"

"Maybe," I said coyly. "My boss is a real piece of work. Very difficult to please. I'm sure there are a whole bunch of butlers here who know exactly what I'm talking about."

I paid for our drinks and we ambled down the nearest corridor.

"They even have a replica of a butler's pantry," I said, indicating the room to my right. "It's empty. Should we go in?"

Jenkins smirked. "You're a bad influence, Miss Rose."

"I'll take pictures for the paper," I said. "Easier to do when there aren't bodies in the way." Living or dead.

We slipped into the room and went to the shelves to check out the magical herbs and spices.

"I feel like you need to have such a vast knowledge of *everything*," I said. "Simon is a font of information. My aunt relies on him heavily."

"Yes, I think the longer the relationship lasts, the more reliant the owner becomes on the butler," Jenkins agreed. "It's a co-dependent relationship at its finest."

"Simon knows what my aunt wants before she does," I said. "Is it like that for you?"

"Not so much," Jenkins admitted.

"My aunt was furious with the sheriff for interviewing Simon about the murder," I said, feigning interest in a row of tonics. Sore muscles. Headaches. Visits by the in-laws. Who didn't need a tonic for that?

"Sounds like she's very loyal to him," Jenkins said.

"It works both ways," I said. "By the way, I spoke to a few other butlers and they mentioned you'd had a dispute with

Higgins during breakfast the morning of the murder. Do you remember?"

Jenkins soured. "Of course I remember. It isn't every day you argue with someone who drops dead a couple of hours later."

"He dropped dead because someone murdered him," I said. "You make it sound as though he keeled over from an aneurysm."

"I didn't mean it that way." Jenkins adjusted his cuff links, clearly uncomfortable with the direction of the conversation. "The argument was nothing. I offered my condolences on the loss of Lottie Stanhope. He then made a less-than-complimentary comment about Mr. Stanhope, so I responded in kind."

"Right. You serve members of the same family."

"Different residences. They have nothing to do with each other."

"So you were defending your respective Stanhopes," I said, smiling. "That's kind of adorable."

Jenkins relaxed. "I suppose it's the butler version of smack talk."

I laughed. "Do you know anything about the map?"

He looked genuinely confused. "What map?"

"Doesn't matter," I said. It was probably best not to mention a treasure map to someone with no knowledge of it. "Was breakfast the only interaction you had with Higgins?"

"Basically," he replied. "He just happened to be in front of me in the line that morning and I heard someone greet him by name. We'd never met prior to here."

"Did you expect him to give you a hard time?" I asked.

"Not particularly," Jenkins said.

"Who started the conversation?" I asked.

"He did," Jenkins said. "Like I mentioned, he made a comment and I rose to the bait. It was a foolish response. I should have brushed it off because I could see he was itching for an argument."

It sounded similar to his uncharacteristic behavior at dinner the night before. Something had obviously been on the butler's mind. Maybe it was the death of Lottie Stanhope. Or maybe it was something else entirely.

"I should probably get back and take notes," I said.

"Thanks for the coffee," Jenkins said. "Will you be dining at Palmetto House again during my stay?"

"Never say never," I said.

Jenkins saluted me with his cup. "I never do."

CHAPTER 9

IT WAS the day of the pack barbecue and I was in complete meltdown mode. I paced the length of the kitchen, debating what to contribute. After the meatloaf massacre, I was afraid to delve into the world of magical cooking. Unfortunately, I left it until the last minute. Procrastination did me no favors.

"I'll stop at the Wish Market," I said. "What's a special dessert for werewolves?"

"It's not a wedding, Rose," the sheriff chastised me. "You don't need to do anything special. Pack barbecues are completely normal. You'll see."

Normal? I was still getting used to the fact that I was a witch and that werewolves existed. Besides, it was one thing to agree to a couple of dates with the sheriff. It was quite another to have to get to know his entire werewolf family.

"I don't know," I said. "We have a killer on the loose. Maybe we should postpone the family meet-and-greet and do something simple like Bailiwick Burgers."

Sheriff Nash patted me on the shoulder. "I appreciate that you're a cheap date, Rose, but a barbecue with the pack will be loads more fun. Trust me. And it'll give you a chance to mingle with the common folk. I mean, not everyone can be lucky enough to be descended from the One True Witch."

Ugh. He definitely had a chip on his shoulder about the Rose clan. I couldn't help my heritage any more than he could help his.

"Just go, Mom," Marley called from her bedroom. "Stop stalling."

"Stop eavesdropping," I yelled back. My daughter clearly needed a lesson on privacy. I glanced helplessly at the sheriff. "At least let me stop at the Wish Market on the way." Store-bought food had to be better than no food at all.

"I already told you, the spread is taken care of," he insisted. "You're meant to come empty-handed. No one's trying to trick you."

I wanted to believe him, but it was hard. I was still reeling from the recent discovery that I was expected to take a hostess gift to my aunt for Sunday dinners.

I stopped pacing. "Okay, no food. Then what does one wear to a pack barbecue?"

The sheriff grinned. "Clothes are a good start, at least until midnight." He winked.

I threw out my hands. "Clothes, perfect. Let me go change. I'll be two minutes."

"She'll be ten minutes," Marley called. "She's incapable of doing anything in two minutes, except rip somebody a new…"

"Marley!" I interjected.

The sheriff chuckled. "Do you think Marley would like to come, too?"

I hesitated. On the one hand, I liked the idea of Marley getting to meet people I was spending time with. On the other hand, it was hard enough for me to agree to go out with someone. I didn't want to drag Marley into a relation-ship unnecessarily. What if the sheriff and I quickly realized that we couldn't stand each other, but Marley had become attached? It was bad enough that she'd taken a liking to Alec. No, it was better to keep Marley out of it.

"Maybe next time," I said.

"If you're sure," the sheriff said. "There'll be plenty of kids at the barbecue for her to play with. That's one thing there's no shortage of in the pack is kids. Wolves love the reproduction process, from start to finish."

"I bet," I said.

"I'm spending the day with Florian," Marley yelled. "He's taking me on the boat to see mermaids."

"Is that for your benefit, or his?" I called. I knew which one my money was on.

I hurried upstairs to change. Not that I had any clue what to wear for a werewolf barbecue. I began to feel nervous. What if they served raw meat? No, barbecue implied that there would be cooking involved. I chose a pair of denim shorts and a blue top with cut out shoulders. Aster said it was the current trend and insisted that I own a top like this.

We dropped Marley off at Florian's man cave and continued driving in the direction of Fairy Cove. It was a beautiful day, which was par for the course in Starry Hollow.

"Where's the barbecue?" I asked. "Your mother's house?"

"Heck, no. The pack owns land that overlooks the sea, so we try to take advantage of it every now and again. We're wolves at heart. We like to be outdoors as much as possible."

"Well, I'm not a wolf, but that's how I feel, too," I said.

"That's the witch in you," the sheriff said. "You have a deep connection to nature, same as us."

"Do you ever wish you were anything else?" I asked.

He looked at me askance. "Anything else? Like what, a vampire? A wizard?" He shook his head firmly. "I can't imagine being anything other than a werewolf. Suits me to a T."

We parked in a clearing where there were already about a dozen vehicles in a row.

"I see my brother's already here," the sheriff said.

"I guess he'll have brought a date, too," I said. Wyatt Nash seemed incapable of going anywhere without one, even when he was married to Linnea.

"Yes, but Bryn and Hudson are here, too," the sheriff said.

Bryn and Hudson had inherited the Nash werewolf gene, much to my aunt's displeasure. Just one more reason she loathed Wyatt.

We threaded our way through the trees until we reached another huge clearing that overlooked the sea. It reminded me of the place where I'd met Iris Sandstone practicing yoga one morning. The High Priestess of the coven also happened to be a dedicated yogi.

"This is pack land?" I queried. "How'd you get so lucky?"

"One of my ancestors was a shrewd negotiator. Or so I'm told."

The wind carried the sound of music to our ears.

"Your cousin's band?" I asked.

"Yep. The Drunk Pandas. They're getting better every time they play. That's why we encourage them." His gaze lingered on my shorts. "You chose a little too well, Rose. I suspect I'll be beating back half the pack today."

The barbecue came into full view as we rounded a corner. As promised, there were tables loaded with food. There were several grills working at the same time, and even a makeshift bar. A round woman with thick brown hair came bustling over when she saw us.

"There you are, Granger. We were wondering when you would show." She fixed me with a broad smile. "You must be Ember. It's so nice to finally meet you. I'm Marianne Nash, Granger and Wyatt's mama."

So this was the woman who gave birth to the Nash brothers. "Thanks for having me today. I've been looking forward to it." The way I looked forward to root canal.

Marianne Nash put her arm around my waist and steered me toward the other werewolves. "Stick with me and you'll be fine. If anyone gets out of line, just give them a good smack on the nose. That's always worked for me."

I glanced at the sheriff over my shoulder. He gave me a cheerful shrug and headed toward the bar. Traitor!

I met more wolves in one afternoon than I'd met during my entire stay in Starry Hollow. Where had they been hiding all this time? I felt like Dorothy in the scene from the *Wizard of Oz* when all the munchkins emerged from the shrubbery at Glinda's behest.

Marianne and I sat at a picnic table to enjoy another round of drinks and grilled food when I decided to broach the subject of Mr. Nash.

"The sheriff...I mean, Granger never talks about his dad," I said, between sips of homemade honeysuckle tea. "Is he not in the picture?"

"Heavens no," she replied. "Roy died when the boys were young."

"I'm sorry," I said quickly. "I didn't realize." Although the sheriff wasn't as guarded as Alec, he was tightlipped about certain aspects of his life. His dad was one of them.

"You never remarried?" I asked.

"Never interested me," she said. "Marriage in general never interested me. Roy was the only reason I dove into the marital pond. I wouldn't do it for anyone else."

"He must've been one-of-a-kind."

"Absolutely. It's still hard sometimes," Marianne admitted. "He had such a big personality. The pack fell apart for a while after his death. It took some time to pull back together."

She didn't offer the details of his death, so I didn't ask.

"I bet he'd be proud of Granger," I said. "Becoming sheriff in a town like Starry Hollow at his age is pretty impressive."

"If it weren't for his daddy's death, I doubt he would've wanted to become sheriff," Marianne said. "It was when they were investigating the murder that Granger became interested in law enforcement. Before that, he was all about athletics."

The murder? "Your husband was murdered?"

Marianne tilted her head. "I'm surprised he didn't tell you. Who am I kidding? He barely tells me anything and I'm his mother."

The sheriff chose that moment to reappear. "And how are you wonderful ladies getting on over here?" He sat beside me and gave my thigh a reassuring squeeze.

"Peachy keen," his mother said. "Ember's life in New Jersey is fascinating. Don't you think?"

It wasn't every day life in the armpit of America was described as fascinating.

"I think everything about Rose is pretty fascinating." He grinned at me.

"How much have you had to drink?" I asked, squinting.

"Werewolf punch is potent stuff," Marianne said. "Designed to overcome our relative immunity to the effects of regular alcohol."

"Designed to get you good and drunk, in other words," I said.

The sheriff chuckled. "It's a barbecue. That's what we do. Eat, drink, and get naked."

"Excuse me?" I almost spit out my honeysuckle tea.

"Oh, he doesn't mean like that," Marianne said. "Granger, don't torment the poor witch." She gave me an easy smile. "We turn and go for a nice run later, after sunset."

"Turn? As in, go full furry?" I queried.

"That's right," Granger said. "It's quite a sight."

"Is that…safe for me?" Or did I need to seek security from the sole werebear in attendance?

"Of course, it's safe," Granger replied. "We're not vampires. There's no bloodlust involved. I secured the permit months ago. Can't have the sheriff's family breaking the rules. I'd never hear the end of it."

"There are animal instincts, though," Marianne said. "You should warn her about those."

"You mean someone might pee on my leg?" I was used to that from PP3.

"I like to think our manners are better than that," the sheriff said. "Except maybe Wyatt's."

His mother swatted his arm. "Granger, be nice. Your brother has his flaws, but that's not one of them." Marianne jerked her head toward the band. "You should ask your date to dance, Granger. She's been sitting idle for too long."

He gave me an appraising look. "How about it, Rose? Ready to shake it with the sheriff?"

"I'm not sure." I glanced at the clearing in front of the makeshift stage where shifters were kicking up their heels and having a blast. Their moves were far smoother than anything I could manage. With my luck, I'd kick one in the shins and the sheriff would have to step in to defend me, swearing up and down that it wasn't an overt act of aggression.

"What're you worried about?" the sheriff asked. "I'll keep my hands to myself." He pretended to tie them behind his back. "You can use my handcuffs if you really don't trust me."

Marianne pressed her hands to her cheeks. "Granger, such talk. Just treat her like the gentleman you are."

"I'm trying, Mama. As you can see, she doesn't make it easy."

I swallowed the last of my tea and stood. "I'll make it easy, but only after a glass of that potent punch."

"Liquid courage," he said, clearly delighted. "Might be a little on the strong side for your delicate constitution." He laughed. "Who am I kidding? I've seen you drink. Come on."

He looped his arm through mine and guided me to the table with the punchbowl. He filled a cup and handed it to me. "Take it slow. You don't want to drink this too quickly."

"She can handle it, brother." Wyatt appeared beside us, his arm thrown casually around the shoulders of a reedy brunette. "One for Micha, too, while you're at it."

Micha's smile seemed too practiced to be genuine. "Only fill mine an inch. I don't need the extra calories." She patted her flat stomach.

"You'll work 'em off at sunset," Wyatt insisted. "Shifting does the body good." He squeezed his date's shoulder. "Micha is a personal trainer. We met at the gym."

"You joined a gym?" The sheriff sounded skeptical.

"No, I was waiting for a date to finish her workout."

"While he was waiting, he met me in the lobby." Micha bumped his hip. "We've been inseparable ever since."

"Since...?" I prodded.

"Yesterday," Micha said, as though it was perfectly obvious.

"That's nice," the sheriff said. "Glad you could make it to the barbecue."

"Our faction of the pack holds its barbecue next month," Micha said. "It's always a good time. You'll love it, Wyatt."

She was dreaming if she thought the relationship would last another twenty-four hours. Didn't every female in the pack know to steer clear of Wyatt Nash?

"You don't have one big pack barbecue?" I queried.

"Too big," the sheriff said. "We wouldn't have the outdoor space needed."

"You could use the convention center," I joked. "Make the

inside like a forest. What they've done for the butler conference is pretty amazing."

The sheriff appeared thoughtful. "You know what, Rose? That's not a bad idea."

"Really? Because I was kidding."

"We could open the roof," the sheriff said. "Use it as an amphitheater so we can still see the moon."

"All that testosterone in a closed environment, though," I said. "Isn't that risky?"

"The convention center uses magic," Wyatt said. "It wouldn't feel closed in. The illusion of a wide open space would seem real." He lightly punched my arm. "I don't care what anyone says, Ember. You've got those Rose brains."

I set my empty punch cup on the table. "They say I don't have the Rose brains?"

"No, of course not," the sheriff said pointedly. "No one says that, do they, Wyatt?"

Micha scrutinized me. "You're a Rose?" She tilted her head up at Wyatt. "As in your ex-wife?"

"Linnea is my cousin," I said. "Speaking of Roses, where are Bryn and Hudson? I haven't seen them."

"Playing tag in the woods with the others," Wyatt said. "After sunset, they'll do it in wolf form. Use their other senses."

"It's great training for other activities," Micha said suggestively.

"When they're much, much older," the sheriff added.

"How old is Bryn?" Micha asked. "I wasn't much older than her when I…"

Even Wyatt couldn't tolerate the conversation. "Bryn is my daughter, Micha. She'll be locked in a tower for another five years."

"Then she'll find a way to sneak out," Micha said. "You can't contain the wolf."

It was like a light switch flicked on in Wyatt's head. "Bryn is a teenager." He examined his date closely. "She's only a few years younger than you."

"More than a few," I said, and quickly covered my mouth. "I mean, Micha's clearly old enough to make her own decisions."

Beside me, Sheriff Nash smirked.

"How many boys are out there with her now?" Wyatt asked.

"Almost all the kids are playing," the sheriff said. "Don't worry about it. She'll be fine."

"How about a dance?" Micha asked, rubbing his bicep.

"Maybe later," he replied. "I'm gonna check on my kids." He unhooked himself from her and stalked off toward the woods.

"I'll come with you," Micha said, chasing after him.

"He doesn't need to be concerned about Bryn," I said. "She's an incredibly bright girl."

"You and I know that," the sheriff said. "But I think it's good to let him worry for a change. Might activate a part of his brain that I thought was long dead."

"Which part is that?" I asked.

"The compassionate part." He eyed me. "Now, how about that dance? The sun will set soon, and I'll need to join the pack."

"What should I do?" I asked. "Hide in the car with the doors locked?" I wasn't sure how I felt about being surrounded by so many naked werewolves in the dark.

"Any interesting spells you could conjure?" he asked. "Full moon and a forest full of furries. Could be fun."

An idea occurred to me. "I could astral project. Run with the pack from the safety of the car."

The sheriff regarded me carefully. "What's that now?"

"I can try to join you. I guess, technically, my consciousness would join you while my body stays behind in the car. That way if animal instincts do get out of hand, I'll be safe." I stifled a yawn. The punch was so potent that it was making me sleepy.

"You'd be safe no matter what, Rose," he said, leaning closer. "I'd never let anything bad happen to you."

"No one can promise that, Granger," I said. "Life taught me that early on. Accidents happen and there isn't a damn thing you can do about it." My head buzzed from the punch, and a yawn escaped me. "I know you'd never put your niece and nephew in danger, though, so it must be safe enough." Then again, Bryn and Hudson were werewolves.

He smoothed back my hair and kissed my forehead. "I'm sorry you've had a rough start in life, Rose. If I could absorb all that hurt and carry it for you, I would."

My heart stirred. There was no denying that Granger Nash was sweet and considerate, unlike Alec. I gave my head a shake. I didn't want to play the comparison game. It wasn't fair. Granger was willing to take a risk and Alec…was not. It was as simple as that.

I retreated to the car in order to prepare for my first pack run. I closed my eyes to focus my mind on astral projection and promptly fell asleep.

CHAPTER 10

"Are all my lessons going to take place in the woods behind my house?" I asked. "I mean, it's convenient location-wise, but a change in environment might be good for me. Stimulate the brain." That's what Marley would say, anyway.

Ian, the perpetually congested Master-in-Familiar Arts, clasped his hands in front of him. "I thought, for the first lesson, your familiar would be more comfortable in his natural habitat. After today, we can resume lessons elsewhere, if you'd be more comfortable."

Raoul tried to fist bump me. *Cool. Someone finally putting me first. About freakin' time.*

"There you are," a take-charge voice said. Marigold came traipsing through the leaves, a determined look in her eye. "I expected you to still be at the cottage."

"You're joining in the lesson?" I asked.

Marigold nodded. "As the Mistress-of-Psychic Skills, you need me to forge the link between your familiar and Ian."

I scrunched my nose. "Why would you need to do that?"

"It assists in making the lesson go smoothly," Ian explained. "If I know what your familiar is thinking, I can help redirect him or address any issues without the need for translation. It makes for a more streamlined process."

I wasn't sure that was such a hot idea. I'd heard some of Raoul's thoughts. I had no doubt they were very different from the thoughts of Precious, my aunt's delicate snowflake of a familiar.

Will I be able to hear his thoughts, too? Raoul asked me.

I raised my hand. "Raoul wants to know if he'll be able to read your thoughts, Ian. Or does it only work in one direction?"

"It will work the same as any familiar bond," Ian said. "So, in short, yes."

Raoul scampered around the ground like he'd discovered a full trashcan. *Woo hoo! I'm going to be able to do something you can't,* he taunted.

I have no interest in reading Rudolph's thoughts, thank you very much, I said.

Rudolph? I thought his name was Ian, Raoul said.

It is, but his shiny red nose automatically conjures up images of the famous reindeer.

Raoul doubled over with laughter. *This is going to be a hoot.*

"Are we ready?" Marigold asked, tapping her foot impatiently.

"What's the rush? You got big plans today?" I asked her.

"As it happens, I do," she said. "Whenever the butler conference comes to town, I get together with a friend. He cancelled our lunch the other day at the last minute, so we've rescheduled for today. I'm just pleased they've extended the conference so he's still in town."

"Ooh. Does Marigold have a love connection with a butler?" I teased. "Does he clear those cobwebs away?"

Raoul fist bumped me again. *I bet he polishes her knockers.*

My brow creased. *Okay, yours crossed the line.*

Raoul shrugged his furry shoulders. *I'm a raccoon. What do you want from me?*

"Smithers and I met here in town the first year he attended the conference," Marigold explained. "We share a similar disciplined approach to life."

Disciplined approach? Raoul echoed. *That either sounds incredibly boring, or incredibly kinky. Hard to tell with this one.*

Marigold took Ian's hand and I cringed. All I could think about was his postnasal drip and how often he must reach for a hanky. I was glad I didn't need to do any handholding.

Marigold wriggled her fingers at Raoul. "Take my hand, please, washbear."

Washbear? Raoul complained. *Not again.*

Hey, at least she didn't call you a trash panda, I said.

"Now, Ian, take Raoul's other hand," Marigold said. They did as instructed. "I'm going to do a quick chant, and then I'll need you to test out the link. Ian, you will ask Raoul telepathically what his favorite color is and then report back the answer. Raoul you will confirm whether Ian is correct."

They both nodded. Marigold performed an incantation, her eyes closed and a serene expression on her usually tense face. A breeze encircled us, kicking up dirt and leaves.

"Brown," Ian said.

"Well, that can't be right," I said. "Marigold, you'll need to try again."

Why? He's right, Raoul said.

"A-ha!" Ian said. "It did work."

"Whose favorite color is brown?" I asked incredulously.

All my favorite things are brown, Raoul said.

I waved my hands emphatically. "No need to elaborate. I get the idea."

You're disgusting, Raoul said.

Marigold dusted off her hands. "My work here is done, then?"

"It is," Ian said. "Thank you for taking time out of your busy day."

As Marigold marched off to her next appointment, Ian's attentiveness didn't escape my attention.

"You like her," I said, once Marigold was out of earshot.

Ian turned his head toward me. "Of course. She's a fine and amiable witch."

Raoul clapped his claws together. *You're right, Ember. He has the hots for her. Amiable, my furry butt.* Raoul clutched his stomach, laughing.

Ian wiped his brow with a handkerchief. "I'm beginning to think this was a bad idea."

"I'm sorry," I said. "You have no idea what you're in for with us. Aunt Hyacinth should never have rushed us into this. We're not ready."

He agrees, Raoul told me.

"Stop translating for me," Ian snapped, and immediately regretted his tone. "I'm terribly sorry. I'm usually better about keeping my guard up around Marigold. It's just that she looked so pretty today. She's a natural beauty and the forest only seems to accentuate her positives."

I suppressed a smile. Marigold, a natural beauty? If you liked that cheerleader meets drill sergeant look, then I guess so. At least it wasn't Hazel he had a crush on. That would cause me to question his sanity.

Hazel's not so bad, Raoul said.

For a crazed clown, no, she isn't, I replied.

Ian looked between us. "You don't like Hazel?"

I groaned. "This link is already a pain in the butt. I like Hazel fine. I like Hazel the way I like medicine when I'm sick. A bitter necessity."

"I suppose we should get started," Ian said. "I know you have quite the busy schedule."

She plans to take a nap after this, Raoul said.

"Raoul!" I said sharply. "I think there's supposed to be some level of trust between a familiar and a witch."

"Too right, Miss Rose," Ian said. "A familiar is far more than a mere companion to a witch. His role is to offer protection and guidance, or even assist with the magical arts."

"Ha! The only place he's going to guide me is to the dump," I said.

Ian ignored my remark. "He can also do your bidding, if requested. In ancient times, they acted as servants. In fact, the name is derived from *famulus*, which is Latin for servant."

I pointed a mocking finger at Raoul. "Ha ha. You're my servant. Do my bidding, trash panda."

"A familiar can also act as a spiritual guide, almost like a guardian angel."

I looked at Ian in disbelief. "You expect my spirit to be guided by an animal whose main goal in life is to inhale as much trash as possible in one sitting? This seems unfair on a very basic level."

Ian blew his nose and tucked the tissue back into his cloak pocket. "I think it would behoove us to work on a trust exercise today. Help the two of you forge a closer bond. Merely having a telepathic link isn't going to foster the type of relationship you should have with your familiar."

"So, what?" I said. "We want to get to a point where he curls up on my lap at dinner like Precious does with Aunt Hyacinth?"

I'd be down with that, Raoul said.

I made a sound of disgust. "In your dreams, street rat."

I am not a rodent, Raoul protested. *Raccoons are in the bear family, hence washbears.*

"Let's begin with a trust walk," Ian said. "Miss Rose will be blinded and it will be your familiar's job to safely guide you to the end of the path."

"I think you mean blindfolded," I corrected him. "You said blinded."

Ian inclined his head. "I'm a wizard. Why should I use a blindfold when magic will do?" He produced his wand and said, "*Caecus.*"

Everything went black.

"Hey, I hadn't agreed to this yet," I objected.

"You don't need to agree," Ian said. "I'm the instructor and you are my student. I will handle the lesson as I see fit."

This guy's growing on me like a fine set of whiskers, Raoul said.

"Raoul, do you see those two live oaks at the end of the path?" Ian inquired.

"I don't," I grumbled.

"Your job is to guide Miss Rose to the end without letting her sustain injuries," Ian continued.

The path looks pretty clear, though, Raoul said. *How hard can it be?*

I heard the sound of a tree falling and a loud thud. Then I heard a crackle and felt the warmth of nearby flames.

"Are you burning down the forest just to teach us a lesson?" I asked.

"Not to worry, Miss Rose. The magic is contained," Ian said. "Go on, Raoul. The path awaits."

Beside me, I felt my familiar hesitate.

What's wrong? I asked.

Um, I'm a little freaked out, he admitted. *Fire and I have a bad history.*

It'll be fine, I reassured him. *Ian won't let anything happen to us. It's only a lesson. Guide me to the end of the path and he'll put everything back like it was.*

Okay. He sounded hesitant. *Take a few steps forward.*

How many is a few? Five?

I don't know, he replied. *Four? Your feet are bigger than mine. I can't judge!*

Calm down, buddy. You're overthinking it.

You're the one demanding exact numbers, Raoul said. *That's what I call overthinking it.*

Ian heaved a sigh. "Perhaps you could act less like siblings and more like spiritual partners."

I forgot Ian was still plugged in. "I'm going to take four steps forward, Raoul."

Okay, the raccoon replied, and I began to walk. *But watch out for that…*

I tripped and nearly fell forward on my knees. Thankfully, I was able to steady myself.

Tree stump, he finished sheepishly.

"Now what?" I asked. "More steps?"

There's a bush with thorns on your left, he said. A*void that. Oh, and it's on fire so don't brush up against it.*

Try not to bury the lead, I suggested. I took a few more tentative steps ahead. The heat from the burning bush nearly singed the hair off my arm. "Why do I get the sudden urge to call you Moses?"

"Ah, a Biblical reference," Ian said, with an awkward laugh. "Very good, Miss Rose."

"At least someone appreciates my humor," I said.

I appreciate it, Raoul said. *When it's funny.*

"Argh," I said. "How many more steps to the end?"

Um, you might want to hop up on the fallen tree, he said.

Why? Suddenly, the ground beneath my feet felt warm and wet.

There might be a little lava issue, he said.

My pulse quickened. "Where's the tree?"

Up here, he said, taking my hand. *I'm already on it.*

Way to save yourself first, I said. *Some spiritual guide you are.*

I put on my oxygen mask first, he argued. *That's parenting 101.*

First, you're not my parent. Second, you're a raccoon. How do you have any knowledge of airline rules?

You'd be surprised what reading materials I come across at the dump, he replied.

I tried to walk along the fallen tree without slipping off. "Is the lava really necessary?" I called over my shoulder. It seemed like overkill for this particular lesson.

Ian didn't respond.

One foot in front of the other, Raoul said. *About three more steps and…*

I lost my footing.

"Grab her, Raoul," Ian shouted.

I felt my familiar reach for me as I tumbled off the tree. His claws sliced my arm but failed to keep hold. I braced myself for a fall.

"What's happening?" Although I couldn't see, I knew I was hovering in mid-air.

"I took action," Ian said.

My vision returned and I immediately saw that the forest was restored to its normal state. No lava. No fire.

"Seems we have our work cut out for us," Ian said. "It's to be expected, I suppose. You're both new to this world, in one way or another."

"Why did you intervene?" I asked.

"Because your aunt would not take kindly to me roasting her favorite niece on the forest floor." He adjusted his collar. "I suspect she would do far worse to me in response."

Sorry, witchy poo, Raoul said. *I'll do better next time.*

Don't you dare call me witchy poo, I said. *I've completely lost faith in you.*

Can't lose something you never had in the first place, Raoul replied.

I ignored him and turned to Ian. "Well, that was a fun lesson," I said. Not. "What's on the agenda for next time?"

"Perhaps some elementals work," Ian said. "And, clearly, more trust exercises."

I'll do better, Raoul said. *Promise. The last thing I would ever want is for Ember to get hurt. She's my purpose in life. Well, her and a full garbage truck after a collection at the grocery store.*

"Will we need Marigold again to create a link between you two?" I asked. "When does this one wear off?"

"This one ends with the lesson," Ian said. "It's a customized spell. And, yes, Marigold will be at the next lesson same as this one." He wagged a finger at me. "I don't need to read your mind to know what you're thinking, Miss Rose. Do not attempt to play matchmaker with us. It's bound to end in tears. I won't say whose."

"Why not?" I asked. "You're both in the coven. That seems to be the most basic requirement."

"We have a history that you know nothing about," Ian said, fishing out his tissue once more.

Yuck. I couldn't imagine kissing that congested face. There was no way you could walk away without a memento of his postnasal drip.

"Somebody needs to read Marigold's mind, to see if she feels the same," I said.

"Good luck trying to forge a connection with the Mistress-of-Psychic Skills without her knowledge," Ian said. "That would take a more advanced witch than yourself." He hesitated. "No offense, of course."

"I know my limitations," I admitted. Wouldn't stop me from trying, though. I was stubborn like that.

"This was a worthy lesson," Ian said. "I look forward to the next one."

I patted him on the shoulder. "I think you're the only teacher that feels that way about me."

"I haven't heard Wren complain," Ian said.

Ooh, the hot wizard, Raoul said. *I still think you're missing out there.*

Thankfully, Ian was already on the path that led out of the woods. A clear path, without lava.

"See you next time, Ian," I called after him, waving.

Once Ian disappeared from view, Raoul turned to me. *We're totally gonna try to do a link with Marigold, right?*

I smiled. *Familiar, this is the beginning of a beautiful friendship.*

After stalking butlers around the convention center for an hour with no leads to show for it, I decided to hatch a plan to trick Marigold into developing a psychic link with me. I wanted to find out more about her history with Ian. It wouldn't be easy to direct her attention to the congested wizard while there was a special friend in town, though. Her disappointment over the cancelled lunch with the butler was apparent. My pace slowed as I realized that their original lunch had been scheduled for the day of the murder. Was there a chance Smithers was involved in the murder and that was the reason he cancelled? Maybe I could catch a killer and remove a romantic rival in one fell swoop. Bonus!

As much as I wanted to go home and curl up in a lazy ball on the couch, I decided to take action. A couple of quick calls revealed that Smithers was a guest at the Kraken Hotel. My phone calls also revealed that the sheriff was busy interviewing staff at the Gryphon, where Higgins had stayed, so I decided to pay a visit to Smithers on my own. I figured if he gave me a hard time, I'd throw some unpolished silverware at him and make a run for it.

Smithers was not the butler I expected to meet. While his name suggested a certain similarity to Ian, the butler himself was buff, bald, and sported an intimidating skull-and-cross-bones tattoo on his bicep.

"You're Smithers?" I queried, darkening the doorway of his hotel room. Although his appearance made me question my plan, I drew comfort from the fact that my wand was safely tucked away in my waistband.

"That's right, love." Smithers' intense gaze traveled down the length of me. "You don't look as strong as the usual girl, but you'll do.

I balked. "Do for what?"

"You're not here to give me a massage?" He flexed his muscles. "My shoulders are a mess. Knots like the ones on a tree trunk."

Arms like tree trunks, too. "No, sorry. You'd be highly disappointed by my massage efforts." I held up a puny arm. "No upper body strength."

"Well, you're not room service," he said, noting the absence of a trolley or tray.

I forced a smile. "I'm a friend of Marigold's." Friend. Reluctant student. Only a slight difference.

His brow lifted. "Oh. I reckon she's pissed that I had to reschedule again."

"You mean even after the cancelled lunch?" There was hope for Ian yet.

"I got caught in an impromptu meeting with Belvedere," he said. "He's the president of our association and the fella talks a blue streak."

"Yes," I said, inflecting my voice with certainty. "She was *very* disappointed to miss you again when your time here is so limited."

Smithers looked me over again. "Why'd she send you? Like I said, you don't look much stronger than a leprechaun's beard."

Although I wasn't familiar with that particular expression, I filed it away for future use in front of Deputy Bolan the next time he scowled in my direction.

"She didn't send me to rough you up," I said. What kind of relationship did these two have? "Besides, I'm a witch. I don't need to look strong to be strong."

"Fair enough. You'd never guess the feats Marigold's capable of just by the look of her."

Once again, I found myself wondering about the nature of their relationship.

"Where are my manners?" Smithers said, shaking his head. "Please come in. I had my lecture on manners only this morning. Seems I wasn't paying close attention." He stepped aside to let me pass through the narrow doorway.

"My name's Ember Rose," I said. "Does that name ring any bells?"

"Rose? Simon's folks?" He was unimpressed. "I hear the owner of Thornhold is a real…"

I held up a hand. "You need to watch what you say. The owner has a way of knowing when someone's disparaging her."

"Disparaging?" He cracked a smile. "That's a mighty big word for a little bird like yourself."

"Are you sure you're a butler?" I asked. Who would employ this guy? He seemed nothing like the other butlers I'd met; probably one of the reasons Marigold liked him. He was the Bad Boy Butler, serving up naughtiness whenever she beckoned and called. I fought the urge to laugh.

"My master's a vampire called Vlad. Original, I know. Owns a place near Big Sur called Velingrad. Gorgeous estate. You should pop 'round if you're ever on the West Coast. The place is surreal."

I watched with interest as he began to polish his bald head with a pristine white handkerchief. "So, why did you miss your initial lunch date? Marigold says you two get together every year."

"Yeah, a real shame, that. I was thrown for a loop when Higgins met the true death. Couldn't manage a social call, even one as intoxicating as Marigold."

I choked on saliva. "Wait. Hold on." I wanted to ask about Higgins, but I couldn't let his remark slide. "You find Marigold *intoxicating*?" Surely, he meant the way cold medicine can give someone night terrors if they abuse it.

"She's like a rare blood type," he said, and laughed. "I've worked for Vlad for so long, I've picked up more than a few of his expressions."

I wondered whether he picked up more than expressions from his vampire master, like maybe a taste for blood. "So, you knew Higgins?"

"Not well, but we meet up here every year, so I knew him enough." Once he seemed satisfied by the shine of his head, he tossed the handkerchief aside. "I heard he was killed for some kind of treasure. Why would he bring treasure to a conference? Makes no sense."

"I'm not sure that's entirely accurate," I said, without offering further details. He didn't mention the map; whether that was a deliberate omission, I wasn't sure. "Where did you go that day instead of lunch?"

He stopped examining his reflection in the mirror and faced me. "That's a very pointed question, Miss Rose. What exactly are you asking me?"

"How did you handle news of the murder?" I asked. "Did you go to the pub and toast his memory? Cry in a bathroom stall?"

"I came here, to my room," he said. "Took a nap. Made an offering to the gods. Showered again to wash off the stench of death."

"Says the guy who butlers for a vampire."

"That's different," Smithers replied. "Higgins was freshly dead and not coming back. He was killed right in front of our eyes." Smithers clenched his hands into fists. "A room full of attentive gentlemen and no one saw what happened. Belvedere's right. We're a disgrace to the association."

Smithers seemed genuinely upset. It was then that I noticed the small stack of books on the bedside table, right next to the alarm clock. I could only read the title on the spine of the top book, but it was enough.

Famous Vampire Pirates in American History.

"Don't be too hard on yourself," I said, averting my gaze. I didn't want him to know that I'd seen the books. "I'm a journalist and I didn't notice anything, either. A story unfolded right in front of my eyes and I have no leads." Except the one standing in front of me.

"Higgins seemed like a decent fella. Can't imagine why anyone would want to off him like that." Smithers stroked his bald head. In fact, he seemed a little obsessed with it.

"Since the conference has been extended," I began, "you should reschedule with Marigold. If you only visit once a year, it'd be a shame to miss the opportunity." Since it was likely the only action Marigold got all year. I felt a momentary pang of guilt over Ian, but Smithers was obviously a meaningless fling. If Ian played his cards right, maybe Marigold wouldn't be interested in meeting up with Smithers next year. Then again, in a toss-up between Ian's sniffles and Smithers' biceps, I knew which one I'd choose.

"I plan to," he said. "I figured she might be upset after I cancelled twice in such a short span of time, though. That maybe she thinks I'm trying to send her a message."

This date was a necessity now. I'd have Marigold poke around in his thoughts and find out whether those books on his nightstand were for more than bedtime reading. If she happened to get lucky at the same time, good for her.

"If you're worried about her saying no out of spite, I can act as an intermediary," I said.

Smithers slipped on his black tails, covering his biceps and tattoos. Now he looked more like a butler. "You'd do that for me?"

"More for Marigold," I said. "She's my teacher. If she's in a good mood for our next lesson, we both benefit."

Smithers shook an amused finger at me. "You're a wily one, aren't you? I bet she has to look out for you."

My smile widened. "You have no idea."

CHAPTER 11

"WHY COULDN'T we just send Simon to get the books we need for our assignment?" Florian asked. He gazed around the interior of the library as though he'd never been here before.

"First, because you should do your own work for class," I said. "And, second, Simon is preoccupied. And I'm sure your mother has a list of chores a mile long for him."

"I don't see why butlers even need a conference," Florian complained. "They do the same job day in and day out. What's to learn?"

"Even if it's just an excuse to brush up on existing skills, or an opportunity to complain about their employers, it's worth it for them. Think of it as a mental health break."

Florian chuckled. "I'm not sure it's a mental health break for mother. She loathes this time of year. She's far too accustomed to having Simon attend to her every need. I found her in the kitchen the other morning, holding an empty martini glass. She wasn't sure what to put in it."

"My vote would be nothing at that hour," I said.

"Florian, Ember. Is there something I can help you with?" Delphine appeared from behind the counter. Her hazel eyes sparkled, probably due to Florian's unexpected presence.

"Hi, Delphine," I said. "We're working on a writing assignment for history class and we could use a little help finding the right resources."

Delphine appeared surprised. "I didn't realize you were both taking the class."

"Ember talked me into it," Florian said. "I decided it wasn't such a bad idea to know more local history, especially now that I'm active on the tourism board."

Of course, he neglected to mention the added benefit of his mother's goodwill. Florian was adept at not looking spoiled and selfish in front of those he wanted to impress. It gave me hope that he deemed Delphine worthy of impressing.

"What's your topic?" Delphine asked. "Then we can narrow down which section to go to."

"We've decided to write papers about vampire pirate booty in Starry Hollow," I said.

"Hidden or found?" Delphine asked.

"Still hidden," I said.

"Makes it more exciting," Florian added. "Maybe there's a chance we can find it."

I shot him a disapproving look. "That's not really the point of the assignment." Then again, I was using the assignment for the multi-pronged purpose of catching a murderer and matchmaking, so who was I to talk?

Delphine offered a shy smile. "I can certainly help with that. Follow me."

We made our way to the second floor where there was a special room labeled Starry Hollow history. It seemed to be in distinct sections.

"I didn't realize there'd been so many books written about the town," Florian said.

"Oh, there have been many," Delphine said. "Starry Hollow is rich in history. I believe your grandfather even has a book in here."

"Grandfather?" I repeated. "As in my grandfather, too?"

Delphine bobbed her head of curls. "That's right. I believe he has a book called *Starry Hollow: Brightly Shining*. I can look up the reference number, if you're interested in seeing it."

Florian lit up. "Marley would love that, wouldn't she?"

I thought it was incredibly sweet that Florian would think of Marley. "Yes, she would, and Elvis knows we could always use another book on deck. Marley burns through them like Tic Tacs."

"I'm going to see if I can find it for her," Florian said. "You two keep going with the pirate booty and I'll be right back."

"I can get the reference number for you," Delphine said. "Make it easier."

Florian waved her off. "No, I got this."

He disappeared between the book stacks and I observed Delphine as she remained fixated on the place where Florian had just been standing.

"So, is this a crush, or is this full-blown l-o-v-e?" I asked.

Delphine snapped to attention. "What? I was only thinking about the reference number."

I laughed. "Witch, please. I recognize that lovesick expression. I've seen it on enough soap operas. I knew you liked him, but I didn't realize exactly how much."

The pink in Delphine's cheeks deepened to a crimson. "It doesn't matter. He doesn't know I exist."

"Of course, it matters. Your feelings always matter," I protested.

"Not to someone like Florian," she said. "He's used to the attention. I'm just one of many adoring faces in the crowd."

"If it's any consolation, I can totally see the attraction. If he weren't related to me, I'd probably be right there with you." As spoiled and selfish as Florian could be, I'd witnessed enough goodness in him to know that he was capable of more. In that sense, I understood why his mother refused to give up on him. I only wish she would stop giving *in* to him.

"I've seen the types of women he prefers to date," Delphine said. "I'm a witch. He never dates witches because he knows that's what his mother wants."

Someone had been taking copious notes. "What if he got to know you first? He might decide it was worth asking you out."

"And how would I manage that?" Delphine asked. "It's a rare occasion that brings him to the library."

I beamed. "He's here now. And if you offer to help him with his assignment, I bet he'd jump at the chance." She'd have to appeal to Florian's lazy side, of course, but that was easy.

"Found it," Florian called, triumphant. He came around the corner, holding a book aloft.

"That's great," I said. "Marley will be so excited." So was I, for that matter. Any new link to the family I never knew was a bonus. "Great news, Florian. Delphine happens to love our topic, so she's volunteered to work with us."

"Excellent," Florian said. He dropped into the seat beside her. "If you provide the research and our resident journalist here provides the writing, that just leaves me to do the learning. I can cope with that."

"Florian, you excel at everything," I said. "If you decided to do the research and writing, you would totally rock this assignment."

"Precisely," he said. "So what's the point? Better to let somebody else have a chance to improve themselves."

I groaned. What was worse was that his logic actually made sense to me. It was the future I worried about for

Marley. That she would become jaded in her studies as she grew older and more accomplished.

"I'm going to hunt down a few books," I said. "Why don't you two discuss the topic in a little more depth? Maybe that will help us decide what to focus on."

I retreated into the stacks and, to my delight, located three books that were actually useful. My disappearance had been a ruse, of course, but a productive one. I called the books down from the shelf by name and tucked them under my arm. My bedtime reading was covered for the next few nights.

When I returned to the table, Delphine and Florian were deep in conversation about the origin of Arctic trolls. Florian stood when he saw me approaching.

"Are you about ready? I have a meeting in half an hour across town."

"This is a good start," I said. "Thanks, Delphine. You've been a great help."

"Anytime," Delphine said. "Let me know when you'd like to come back and I'll make sure my schedule is clear."

Florian winked at her in his usual flirtatious manner. "I'll be in touch."

I waited until we were exiting the building to comment. "I was right about her, wasn't I? I told you she was smart."

Florian stretched his arms over his head and basked in the warmth of the sun. "I never disputed her intelligence. It was her suitability as a date that I questioned."

"Why do I get the feeling that you've changed your mind?" I asked.

"It's not that I've *changed* my mind, so much as I've decided to have an open one. It's hard to resist a girl who knows about Arctic trolls *and* looks at you with those big eyes."

"Sounds like a winning combination to me," I said.

"Too bad she's a witch," he added, and my excitement quickly deflated. Clearly, it would take more than one enjoyable conversation to convince Florian that Delphine was worth his consideration. Luckily for Delphine, I was up for the challenge.

"I've been thinking about these treasure maps," Florian announced. "Ember and I are writing papers about local legends and, I have to be honest, the topic is fascinating."

We were gathered in the main room of the tourism board office, having an impromptu meeting with Aster and Thaddeus.

"Really? You're actually writing a paper? Using actual words?" Aster asked, tapping her elegant fingers on her phone. Her gaze was riveted to the screen and I was surprised she'd even registered Florian's statement.

"I am. I also thought we might incorporate more of the local legends into our promotional efforts," Florian suggested. "Focus more on the vampire pirate history and lost treasure. Tourists would eat that up."

Aster finally glanced up. "To what end? Encourage treasure hunters? I'm not certain those are the sort of paranormals we're interested in attracting."

"You sound like Mother," Florian huffed.

"Simply because I don't agree with you doesn't make me like Mother," Aster snapped.

Florian folded his arms. "As a matter of fact, it makes you exactly like Mother."

Aster narrowed her icy gaze before returning her attention to the phone. "Sterling is meant to be home with the boys, but the piano teacher says he hasn't arrived. Naturally, he's not answering my texts."

Florian and I exchanged concerned looks.

"Maybe he's stuck in a meeting," I said.

"He's always stuck in a meeting," Aster shot back and tucked away her phone. "The boys have practically forgotten what he looks like." She suddenly seemed embarrassed to have lost her cool. "I'm exaggerating, obviously."

"You know, Marley and I have been talking about spending more time with the twins," I said. "We'd be happy to babysit one evening, so you and Sterling could have dinner together."

"Alone?" Aster queried.

"That would be the idea," I said. "It seems like you two have been ships passing in the night lately."

She sighed and leaned her elbows on the nearby display table. "I suppose we have. We're both so busy. If it's a choice between spending quality time with the boys and spending time with me, I'm always going to want him to work the boys into his schedule."

Thaddeus pushed up his glasses, a sign he was preparing to speak. "When I was a young centaur, my parents made sure to have time carved into the schedule for each other. They considered their relationship to be the heart of the family. It was their belief that if they kept it beating, then that, in turn, would keep all the other organs thriving. I liked to think of myself as the kidney. It was my favorite organ."

I wasn't sure how to respond to that. No child I knew had a favorite organ.

"We used to make time for each other," Aster admitted. "He would often come home in the middle of the day to have lunch with me. That hasn't happened for ages."

"Is this because the pressure of his job is getting to him?" I asked. It wasn't like Aster and Sterling needed money or prestige. They already had plenty of both.

"That's what I've assumed," she said.

"You haven't discussed it?" I asked. I realized how judgmental it sounded, but it was too late.

"We don't all live filter-free lives, Ember," Aster said. "Sometimes it's best to keep the peace. I see so little of him that I don't want to spend those precious moments arguing about his absence."

No one mentioned the possibility of an affair, but I knew we were all thinking it. No psychic link required for that one.

"Like I said, Marley would love the chance to hang out with the boys again," I said. "And I'd be there to maintain order. Just let me know when."

Aster offered a grateful smile. "Thank you, Ember. That's kind of you. Perhaps we'll take you up on it." She grimaced. "Right now, I'd like him to get home and relieve the piano teacher."

"I'm interested in your idea about the treasure maps, Florian," Thaddeus said, deftly steering the conversation back to business. "What did you have in mind?"

Florian's enthusiasm was palpable. It felt as though all the negative energy in the room immediately dispersed. "We could base the treasure on real stories and design fake maps to correlate with them. Use local businesses as locations on the map to encourage tourists to stop in."

"But it would be clear the treasure isn't real?" I clarified.

Florian shrugged. "We can't say for certain that it isn't. We'd try to be as accurate as possible, maybe bring Delphine or Maisie on board as a consultant." He grinned. "Or both."

I groaned inwardly. Florian could turn any project into a dating strategy, not that he needed one. He only had to ask.

"Delphine is the librarian, isn't she?" Aster asked. "The quiet, pretty witch?"

I jumped right in. "Yes, that's her. Very knowledgeable, too. She's helping Florian and I with our history papers."

"That's where I got the idea," Florian said. "That history class is paying dividends. Such a good idea, Ember."

"I admit I was skeptical when you mentioned attending the class," Aster told her brother. "I was sure there was a woman involved."

"What makes you think there isn't?" Florian countered.

"Delphine isn't your type," Aster said. "She's far too appropriate."

"And Dr. Timmons is, shall we say, a wee bit older than your usual date," Thaddeus added.

"Good thing I'm there to learn, isn't it?" Florian said. "Will you do me a favor and mention to Mother how my history class has added value to the tourism board?"

Aster moaned. "Can you possibly do *anything* without a selfish motive?"

"Does it matter?" Florian asked. "You're benefitting from my selfishness and no one's getting hurt by it."

He made a good point. "I think we should consider his idea," I said. "If you market it the right way, maybe you would attract a broader range of tourists than just treasure seekers. Promote it as old-fashioned family fun or something."

Aster tapped her slender fingers on the table. "The whole idea is growing on me. Let's talk more about it later." Her phone buzzed and she whipped it out of her pocket. "Thank the gods. Sterling's home." Some of the tension faded from her body language and I realized how affected she'd been by his tardiness.

"Text him now and ask him about dinner one night this week," I said.

Aster's expression darkened. "Oh, I don't want to bother him when he only just arrived home. The boys will be climbing all over him."

"He doesn't have to commit now," I said, nudging her. "Just float the idea."

"I suppose it can't hurt." She shot off a text. "You're very sweet to offer. I know how busy you are. I'm not a single mother, but I can imagine the difficulties."

"Marley is old enough now that it's not so bad," I said. "Your boys are still at needy ages. It must be hard to not have that second pair of hands around."

Aster seemed to feel the weight of everyone's stares. "I have plenty of help if I need it. And Sterling is an excellent husband and father. It's only a temporary distraction…whatever it is."

I couldn't decide who she was trying to convince more.

The phone buzzed again. "Sterling says he'll need to check with his assistant." Aster tried to suppress her disappointment.

"Okay, just text me with a date and, hopefully, we can make it work," I said. Marley needed marital role models and I was in no position to help. With me a widow, Linnea divorced, and Florian a content bachelor, it was up to Aster to represent the happily married couple faction, and I was willing to do whatever I could to keep their marriage intact.

CHAPTER 12

"CAN we skip the usual lesson today?" I asked.

Marigold and I were in Rose Cottage, preparing to tackle more telekinesis.

"So you can what? Nap on the sofa?" Marigold clapped her hands. "Time is precious, Ember. You want to grip the day by its lapels. Make the most of it."

"And how is moving a fork across the table with my mind making the most of today?"

Irritation marked her features. "It's a building block."

"What I need is for you to make the most of your time," I said, "with Smithers."

She perked up immediately. "Time with Smithers? What on earth do you mean?"

"You have another plan to meet up with him, right?"

"Yes, today, as a matter of fact." Marigold narrowed her eyes. "How do you know that?"

"Lucky guess," I said. "When you're with him, I need you to take a quick peek in his head, rummage around in his thoughts."

She reeled back. "Heavens no. I couldn't possibly."

I sighed. "We need to rule him out as a suspect. If you could poke around in his mind and find out why he's reading books about famous vampire pirates, that would be a tremendous help."

She steadied herself with a hand on the table. "Smithers is a suspect? Nonsense. He's as forthright as they come. I've known him for years."

"Just one look," I pleaded. "We need to know whether the books are a hobby or something more sinister. You can help us cross his name off the list."

Marigold paused. "If he did happen to stay on the list, would he need to remain in town indefinitely?"

Oh no. "Marigold, you do *not* want Smithers to be a suspect just so you can play banana in the fruit salad."

She cocked her head. "Is that a human world phrase? Why do so many sex euphemisms involve food?"

"I don't know. Hunger?"

She gave me an indulgent smile. "Smarter than you look, Ember."

"Um, thank you?"

Marigold folded her arms. "But I'm not going to do it."

"What? Why not?"

"Because it's an invasion of privacy and trust. Do you have evidence that Smithers was involved aside from his choice of literature? Because if being a history buff is a crime now, I guess you and Florian should be suspects, too. I already thought Florian enrolling in a community college class was suspicious."

"That's completely unrelated," I insisted. "Besides, Smithers had opportunity."

"So did a hundred other butlers at the convention center when Higgins was killed. Will I be reading all of their minds, too?"

"Fine. Forget it," I grumbled. "I was also hoping that you

could show me how to do that linking spell. That way, you don't have to show up for my lessons with Ian, since I could tell it made you uncomfortable." *Smarter than I look, indeed.*

Marigold pursed her lips. "It would be nice to shift that responsibility. It's a disruption to my routine. Slotting in your psychic skills lessons was hard enough, but Hyacinth insisted."

"I'm a fast learner," I said. "Must be those Rose genes."

Marigold considered me. "You did pick up astral projection at an impressive pace. It strikes me as odd that Hazel complains so often." She clamped her hand over her mouth.

"I don't need psychic skills to know that," I said. "Hazel and I don't see eye-to-eye on the importance of the Big Book of Scribbles. A clash is inevitable."

Marigold visibly relaxed. "Let's do it then. Your aunt will be pleased to hear you've advanced in at least one area." She held out her hands.

"No wands?" I queried.

"Not for this," she said. "Many psychic skills don't involve wands."

"Let me get Raoul," I said. "He's outside."

"How do you know?"

I tapped the side of my head. "Familiar bond." And because I told him to wait there until I called him.

Raoul climbed through the open kitchen window and joined us in the living area. Thankfully, PP3 was asleep on my bed. One of the advantages to an older dog with hearing loss.

I took one of Marigold's hands and one of the raccoon's paws.

"You don't actually need Raoul to form the link," Marigold said. "He can watch and learn, but the link between us will essentially pass to him, like a hall of mirrors, since he can already read your thoughts."

"Only when I want him to," I said. "I've gotten better at cloaking." Thanks to Alec.

Raoul seemed disappointed to be left out. He went to the corner and sulked.

"You need to focus your will, as always," Marigold said. "It's very important because you need to connect to the right mind. You won't always have the luxury of being the only ones in the vicinity and you don't want to end up in the wrong head. Trust me, been there, got the psychiatric ward visit."

That sounded…unpleasant.

"There are several options to choose from," Marigold continued, "although I prefer *connectio*. It seems to form the quickest, most adhesive link. It's like a hook and eye, if you don't line it up just so, it slips away."

"Got it," I said. "And how do I unlink?"

"The link is not designed to be permanent," she said. "It'll fade once you've been physically apart for a reasonable amount of time."

"Should I try now?"

"Yes, yes," Marigold said. "May as well see if you can follow instructions."

I closed my eyes, focused my will, and said, "*Connectio*." I felt the shift this time, like a door opening in my mind.

Well done, grasshopper, Marigold said.

My eyes popped. *I did it!* I was so pleased that, for a moment, I forgot the whole reason I forged the link in the first place.

"This is a special skill to be used carefully and respectfully," Marigold said.

"Of course," I said. "Ian gave me a whole lecture on it." A lie that I shielded from Marigold.

"Ian." She sighed heavily and released my hands. "He's very by the book, isn't he?"

"So?" I said. "You're a stickler, too." I tried to concentrate on her thoughts.

"Which is why I prefer someone who isn't," Marigold said. "I don't need someone else with a critical eye and a can-do attitude. I already have me for that. I need more of a balance."

Like Smithers, she thought to herself. *He's the perfect antidote to all that...exactness. Plus, he's built like a fine-tuned machine.*

Couldn't blame her for finding those qualities attractive. Of course, *murderer* might negate all that.

"Ian mentioned you two had a history," I said. "Anything you care to share?"

Her cheeks grew flushed. "Absolutely not. It was a long time ago and not worth mentioning." *And I prefer to steer clear of him. No need to dredge up the past with every encounter.*

Hmm. There was definitely a story there. I listened again, but heard nothing. Stupid hook and eye! I didn't think I'd lose the link so quickly. I only had a tiny window of opportunity to eavesdrop. If I couldn't do it, I needed someone who could. Fast. There was only one paranormal that fit the bill, although I hated to ask him.

"What time are you meeting Smithers?" I asked.

Marigold checked her watch. "Fifteen minutes, so I should go. His hotel is halfway across town."

"I'm headed to the newspaper office," I said. "Would you mind dropping me off on your way?"

"Not at all."

Marigold left me on the sidewalk in front of *Vox Populi* and continued to the hotel. I hurried inside to see if Alec was around. If Operation Eavesdrop was going ahead, then we needed to hurry.

I knocked on the closed door of Alec's corner office. We'd been successfully avoiding each other since his return. It was my understanding that Holly was still in town and I intended to give them a wide berth.

"Come in," came the muffled reply, and I flung open the door.

"Alec, I need you," I said, and suddenly wanted to snatch back those particular words. "I mean, can you help me with an urgent project?"

Alec studied me. "Why do I get the sense that this urgent project involves the potential for trouble?"

I flashed an innocent smile. "Because you know me so well?"

Alec only hesitated a moment before rolling back his chair. "Where are we going?"

"To the Kraken Hotel," I said.

He cocked an eyebrow. "Pardon?"

"Don't worry. We're not getting a room. We'll eavesdrop from the hall."

"We cannot eavesdrop from the hall," he said in a clipped tone. "If you intend to listen properly, we shall need to do it from an adjacent room."

He sounded like he had eavesdropping experience--a question for another day. "Then I guess we're getting a room. We can expense it, right?"

Alec guided me out of his office. "Perhaps we should worry about that later. If the matter is as urgent as you suggest, we need to move swiftly."

I was relieved that Alec was willing to help without too much resistance. I didn't know where I stood with him these days, other than he wanted as little to do with me as possible.

"I wish I had my own broomstick," I said, as we stood outside the office building. "I could get us there in a heartbeat."

"You've earned your license?"

"Not yet," I said. "But Florian is giving me lessons and he says I'm a natural."

Alec offered a vague smile. "That's excellent, Miss Rose. I'm pleased for you."

My spirits lifted. It wasn't every day that Alec made a heartfelt remark, not unless he was under a spell.

"While I can't fly, it'll be faster if I can carry you," Alec said.

Of course. Vampire speed. "That won't look weird to passersby?"

"They won't even register us," he said. "Up you get."

I looped my arms around his neck and he held me against his chest as he sprinted to the hotel at a rapid clip. We arrived so quickly, I was reluctant to let go so soon. Then I remembered the importance of eavesdropping on Smithers and I got my head back in the game.

"We need the room next to 302," I said, as we hurried into the lobby.

We approached the reception desk and Alec gave the elf an engaging smile. "Good afternoon, miss. My girlfriend and I are here to celebrate our anniversary and we were hoping that room 304 is available, for nostalgic reasons."

The elf sighed dreamily. "How nice." She checked her computer screen. "Oh, I'm so sorry, but that room's taken. There's a conference in town that's been extended and we're dreadfully busy."

I elbowed him in the ribs. "Darling, you're such a knucklehead. Our room was 300." I looked at the elf and rolled my eyes. "How quickly they forget."

She shot me a sympathetic look as she checked her computer screen. "You're in luck. Room 300 is available."

"Great," I said. "Could you make it fast?" I linked my arm

through Alec's and squeezed. "It was a long ride to get here and we're in a hurry, if you know what I mean."

I felt Alec stiffen beside me. He reached for his wallet and handed the elf his business credit card.

The elf gave me the key and I dragged Alec to the elevator.

"Why do I get the feeling this is what you would actually be like if the circumstances were real?" he said with a trace of amusement.

I felt a rush of warmth—it was nice to hear Alec speak to me like a friend rather than an associate. I nearly offered a flirtatious reply but bit my tongue. I didn't want to reopen those wounds. Not when they hadn't had time to heal.

We rode up the elevator in silence. It was a smaller, older elevator, and I was very conscious of Alec's body close to mine.

"You'd think they'd have a magical elevator like the one at the Lighthouse," I said, in an effort to diffuse the tension.

"The tension is only in your imagination, Miss Rose," Alec said.

Sweet baby Elvis. I was so focused on the task at hand, that I'd forgotten to put up my mental shield.

"Third floor," I announced, a tad too loudly.

The doors opened and we stepped into the corridor. I turned left, remembering the way to Smithers' room.

"Is this a crime in progress, by any chance?" Alec asked in a hushed tone.

"No, but if you listen closely, you might pick up information on the butler's murder." I knew Marigold wouldn't be able to resist asking about Higgins and the books. I'd planted the seeds. Now it was time to see if anything grew.

We crept into room 300 and clicked the door quietly closed behind us. No need to alert the next room to new neighbors.

Alec strode across the room for a glimpse at the view. "Not very exciting."

"No one books this place for the view," I said. "It's centrally located for the conference and the restaurants."

"I suppose."

I pressed my ear to the wall and struggled to listen.

Alec regarded me. "We're not checking up on your boyfriend, are we, Miss Rose?"

"My boyfriend?" I sputtered. "The sheriff is *not* my boyfriend. And this is official business, I swear."

His hand rested on my shoulder. "It's quite acceptable if he is your boyfriend, Miss Rose. There's no need to hide your romantic life from me, unless you're uncomfortable with your boss knowing personal details of your life."

I pressed my cheek against the door, unwilling to face him. "Is this because of Holly?"

"No, Holly is irrelevant," he said. "It's as we've previously discussed. Nothing has changed." He moved to stand beside me. "What would you like me to focus on?"

"The name Higgins," I said. "Anything connected to the murder at the conference. Thoughts of treasure or a map. A butler named Smithers is in there with Marigold, and I'm willing to bet good money the topic comes up."

Alec's breath was hot on the curve of my neck, resulting in an involuntary shiver. I couldn't think straight with his body so close to mine.

"Cold, Miss Rose? Perhaps you can adjust the thermostat."

"I'm fine," I mumbled. "Just listen so you don't miss anything."

His lips twitched. "They're talking about their missed engagement. A lunch."

Ooh, perfect. "Anything about Higgins?" I jostled him.

He put a finger to his lips. "Quiet, please." He cleared his throat. "Smithers' thoughts are as you would expect."

I shot him a quizzical look. "Is he admiring his bald head in the mirror again?"

"He's admiring something, but it's not a part of his own anatomy."

"Ugh. Marigold?" I tried to block the image from my mind. "What about her? Has she mentioned Higgins yet?"

"Miss Rose, stop talking and I shall tell you."

I pretended to zip my lip.

"His thoughts are centered around undressing her at the moment," Alec said. "I'm not certain that even mention of Higgins can derail his mental process."

"What about hers?" I asked. "If she's not on the same page, then maybe there's still a chance." I leaned into him without thinking and quickly snapped to attention.

Alec ignored my unconscious gesture. "She's debating whether to bring up the subject of Higgins. She thinks he's innocent, but has a sense of guilt for not using her powers to assist you."

"Really?" That surprised me.

"He's about to make a move," Alec said. "He's deciding between a kiss or a grope."

"I think she'd settle for either one," I said. "I get the impression it's been a while."

Alec stifled a laugh. "Yes, I think you are correct in that assumption. She's thankful to be wearing her pink satin undergarments."

I titled my head toward him. "I'm surprised you're willing to do this. It doesn't make you feel bad, eavesdropping on their private moment?"

"I certainly wouldn't do it under normal circumstances," he said. "But you claimed it was a matter of urgency and I trust you."

"You do?" Not that he knew I was to blame for his personality change under the opposite spell.

He bent his head closer. "Of course I do. Why wouldn't I?"

My pulse quickened as I stared at those sensual lips. When would I stop being so attracted to him? Couldn't I settle into a nice professional relationship with him without the angst?

"Higgins!"

I glanced at Alec sharply. "What about him?"

Alec shot me a quizzical look. "I didn't say anything." He put his fingers to his lips.

I closed my eyes and listened.

"I didn't realize you were interested in vampire pirate history." It was Marigold's voice, light and airy. *Please don't be a murderer*, she thought to herself. *You're far too handsome for prison.*

I was still connected to her! My eyes flew open and I gripped Alec's arm. "You listen to his thoughts and I'll listen to hers," I whispered.

Although he seemed mildly confused, he nodded.

"I'm not usually," Smithers replied. "The topic came up so much because of the murder, I decided to read up on it while I was stuck here as a way to pass the time." There was a pause. "When I'm not with you, that is."

Alec leaned toward me. "The butler is telling the truth." He continued to listen intently. "He liked Higgins. Hopes the murderer is caught before he leaves town. He also wants to make the most of his time with Marigold. I don't believe he's your killer, Miss Rose."

Relief washed over me. I didn't love the idea of Marigold being involved with a killer. At least we were next door to rescue her, if the need arose.

"Smithers, you naughty butler." *Do it again.*

Uh oh. How did I unlink myself from Marigold's thoughts?

"You like that, do you?" Smithers asked.

Alec squeezed his eyes shut. "I think it's time to go, Miss Rose. I suddenly feel quite nauseous."

"Same," I croaked. If Alec could've leaped from the window without incident, I think he would have. Some thoughts were better left unheard.

"Indeed," Alec said, as we escaped the room.

"Dammit, stay out of my head," I demanded. "It's already too crowded in there."

Alec smothered a laugh. "You may not believe it, but I have missed you, Miss Rose."

I inhaled sharply. "I've missed you, too."

We left the hotel together in silence, and it was a relief to be back in my own thoughts instead of someone else's.

CHAPTER 13

"You look nice, Sterling," I said. Not that a guy needed to do much to leave the house. A clean pair of trousers and a shirt and we fawned over them like it took a Herculean effort.

Sterling tweaked his cufflinks. "Thank you, Ember. And thanks to you and Marley for offering to watch the boys. We never think to make arrangements in advance. Our schedules are both so hectic."

"I know," I said. "But you have to prioritize your family." You never knew how long you had with them. It sounded too maudlin to say aloud, so I kept my reasons to myself.

I heard Aster at the top of the stairs. "Put the cat down, Ackley. She doesn't like to be held at that angle."

Uh oh. I glanced at Sterling for his response, but his gaze was riveted to his phone. That was no bueno. If he placed that phone on the table at dinner, it was going to be a major bone of contention. I had Aster's number. If there was an issue while they were gone, I'd call her. No need for Sterling to have his phone.

Aster came downstairs and immediately noticed her

husband's face buried in a screen. He didn't bother to glance up.

"Ready?" he asked, barely registering her.

"I need the bathroom first."

"You always look so beautiful," I said. She'd clearly made an effort with her hair and makeup, not that she needed to go the extra mile. Aster was stunning with bedhead and in fuzzy pajamas.

"Mmm," Sterling added.

Although Aster hid the sting of rejection, I sensed her bitter emotion. There had to be a way for Aster to reclaim her husband's attention. Sterling had to realize how lucky he was to be married to someone like Aster. She was the dream wife, there was no denying it.

"I'm going to say goodbye to the boys." Sterling draped his jacket over the back of the chair and set his phone on the table before disappearing upstairs.

I stared at the phone, the gears clicking away in my mind. Did I dare? I only had a minute to act before one of them returned to the room. I pulled out my wand and aimed it at the phone. When the time came to focus my will, I stalled. I had no idea what to do. Make it invisible? Blow it up? Both were too obvious.

"Aspen, the cat doesn't like to wear the shower curtain," Sterling called. "Please take it off and ask Marley to hang it back up."

Oh no. He was coming. My wand shook as I desperately tried to think of a spell. Any spell.

"*Anima,*" I said, and thrust my wand back into my waistband.

"Did you say something?" Sterling asked, returning to the living room.

"Just practicing spells out loud," I said. "So hard to keep track of all my lessons these days."

141

"You should tell your aunt you need a break," he said. "Life can't be all about witchcraft."

"I can handle it," I said. I watched nervously as Sterling tucked his phone in his pocket and slipped on his jacket. What had I done? It was a phone not a garden gnome. It wasn't like it could spring to life.

Aster emerged from the other room, a bright smile plastered across her perfect features. She was determined to make the best of this evening, I could tell.

"We won't be late," Aster said. "I'm sure Sterling has an early start in the morning."

He slipped on his jacket. "You know me so well."

They left the house without touching. I noticed that he didn't give her a peck on the cheek, or place a hand on the small of her back. Not a single intimate gesture. There was no sign of affection between them.

"Enjoy," I called. The door closed and I felt a heaviness in my heart. I hoped whatever I'd done to the phone wouldn't make matters worse between them. Just because a couple wasn't outwardly fighting didn't mean everything was fine. Or maybe it meant that it was no better than fine, a low bar if ever there was one.

The kids came barreling down the stairs, reminding me what my priority was for the evening. Three children + twelve limbs intact + no one loses an eye = success.

"Who wants a snack?" I asked.

"I have allergies," Aspen said. At least I thought it was Aspen. I was never entirely sure. I wished they sported name labels on their foreheads, or something.

"What kind of allergies?" I asked. I didn't recall any issues at our Sunday dinners.

He began counting on his fingers. "Wisteriaberries, fazzlefruit, magic herbs in the purple family…"

"You're allergic to a color?" I queried.

"I believe him," Marley said solemnly. "If it were a lie, he'd have said all vegetables in the green family."

True. "Okay, what do you normally have for a snack?"

Marley lowered her voice. "Isn't it a little close to dinner?"

I glanced at the clock. "Oh, crap. Sorry. Forget the snack."

Aspen promptly burst into tears. "You promised." He wiped his snot away with the back of his hand. "And you said 'crap.'"

I kneeled in front of him. "Technically, I didn't promise. I merely mentioned the possibility."

"It was an implied promise," Marley said.

I glared at her. "Whose side are you on?"

Marley gestured to the sobbing child. "The obvious choice."

"Does he pack your school lunch every morning?" I asked.

"No, but neither do you."

Right. "Well, does he let you sleep in his bed?"

Aspen's waterworks dried up as quickly as they started. He stared at Marley, wide-eyed. "You still sleep with your mom?"

Marley gulped, feeling the weight of a four-year-old's judgment. "Only if I've had a bad dream."

Aspen pointed and laughed. "You sleep with your mom! I'm younger than you and I don't need to do that."

Marley pursed her lips and gave me dagger eyes. "You had to go there."

I shrugged. "He stopped crying, didn't he?"

"Because you threw me under the crybaby bus," Marley shot back.

I clapped my hands once. "Okay. What's for dinner?"

"Don't you already know?" Ackley asked, appearing on the bottom step. "Mommy always knows ahead of time."

Of course she did. She was Aster Rose-Muldoon, pure perfection and obvious descendant of the One True Witch. I was Ember of Maple Shade, New Jersey, First of Her Name, Queen of the Turnpike, and Macaroni and Cheese in a Box.

"I'm learning to use magic to cook," I said. *Just don't request meatloaf.*

"Mommy doesn't use magic to cook," Aspen said. "She wants this to be a magic-free household as much as possible."

"Well, my whole life has been magic-free up until recently," I said. "So I get special dispensation in your house."

Ackley and Aspen exchanged excited glances.

"Can we help?" Aspen asked.

"Sure." I shot a helpless glance at Marley, who merely shrugged. "Let's go into the kitchen and see what kind of mess we can make."

The twins fist bumped each other and followed us into the kitchen. They sat on stools at the counter and watched me expectantly.

"How about chocolate cake?" Ackley asked.

"For dinner?" I asked in disbelief. "I might look young, but I wasn't born yesterday."

Ackley blinked. "You don't look young."

I gritted my teeth. "It's an expression, kid."

Marley swallowed a laugh. "How about snazzlewick squares?"

I elbowed her. "I don't even know what that is."

"They serve it at school sometimes," she said. "It's one of those rare meals that's both popular and healthy."

"Like a unicorn," I said.

Marley frowned. "A unicorn is not a meal."

Right. "I meant the rare part."

"Daddy likes things cooked well done," Aspen offered.

"I don't want to eat a unicorn," Ackley said, and I could detect the onslaught of tears if I didn't react quickly.

"Snazzlewick squares!" I cried. "Give me one second." I produced my wand and stared at the empty counter. I didn't need runecraft. What I needed was a useful class like How To Whip Up A Sensible Meal Before A Four-Year-Old Cries.

I focused my will and poured my energy into the wand, imagining a snazzlewick square. The problem was that I had no frame of reference.

"*Partum*," I said.

"Ew, what's that?" Aspen asked, studying the greenish brown blob that appeared on a plate.

"No clue," I said. "Marley, any ideas?"

Marley poked the blob with a cautious finger. The blob wiggled and she quickly recoiled.

"Awesome," Ackley breathed, his eyes wide.

The blob shifted and tipped off the plate.

"Blob on a stick," I said. "It's moving."

Naturally, Viola picked the worst possible time to appear in the kitchen. The yellow cat immediately zeroed in on the moving blob and began batting it between her paws.

"Viola, no," I scolded the cat. "I don't even know what it is." What if it was poisonous?

The cat ignored me and kept treating the blob like a toy.

"Maybe you should get rid of it," Marley suggested. "What if it…?" She didn't get a chance to finish her sentence. The blob, however, seemed to know exactly what she was thinking as it divided in half.

"No way!" Aspen yelled. "Two blobs."

"No, no, no," I muttered in a panic.

The cat continued to pursue one blob, while the other blob made its way across the counter, leaving a trail of greenish brown goo in its wake.

"Marley, call a friend," I ordered. "Someone has to know what this stuff is."

Ackley disappeared from the kitchen, only to return with a toy bow and arrow. He aimed at the second blob and fired. The arrow pierced the blob and split it in half.

"Three blobs!" Aspen shouted.

I stared at the lines of goo that were now crisscrossing all over the counters. The cat knocked her blob to the floor and jumped down to continue the game.

"Viola, stop," I said firmly. "You're making it worse."

The twins were laughing hysterically now. Marley had her phone out and was taking photos.

"Why are you taking pictures?" I asked, exasperated.

"I'm posting them on a site called Spellcraft," she explained. "I've asked for help identifying them."

"Oh." I paused, holding out my wand without a clue what to do next. "Any comments yet?"

"Yes," she said excitedly. "MagicMax551 says it's a congeros."

"Great," I said. "It has a name. Now how do we get rid of them?"

The original blob divided again and the cat looked quizzically as they parted in different directions, unsure which one to pursue.

Marley typed a plea for help and waited for a response.

"For the first time in my life, I wish I was a Star Trek fan," I complained. Karl used to enjoy it, but I didn't have much interest in science fiction. I had enough cultural awareness to remember *The Trouble with Tribbles* episode.

"What's Star Trek?" Marley asked.

"Look up *The Trouble with Tribbles* and see how they get rid of them at the end," I urged, trying to prevent the blobs from escaping the kitchen.

"Wait, MagicMax551 says to throw salt on them," Marley said.

I ran for the salt shaker on the table. "What will salt do?"

"No idea," Marley said. "Just try it."

"Aspen, no!" I watched in horror as he brought his foot

down hard on the blob on the floor. It immediately splattered into four new blobs.

I chased the blobs around the room, sprinkling salt everywhere I could.

"It's snowing," Ackley said, dancing happily around the kitchen.

The cat became fascinated by the salt and kept trying to lick it off the floor.

"Marley, take the cat upstairs and lock her in a room until this is done," I said.

Aspen appeared behind me with a familiar wand. "I do it."

"Aspen, how did you…?" I felt my waistband. Yep, the little thief had lifted my wand without me even realizing it.

He giggled and waved my wand around the room, taunting me.

"They're melting," Ackley cried, pointing.

I shifted my focus back to the blobs. Sure enough, the salt was dissolving them. I wiped my brow. "Thank sweet baby Elvis."

"Who's Elvis?" Aspen asked.

I wiggled my fingers. "Give me back my wand and I'll tell you."

Aspen tapped the wand on his head, debating the value of the exchange. "No."

Why did his refusal not surprise me? "Okay then. How about you give me my wand and I'll let you stay up half an hour past your bedtime."

"Hour," he said.

I pretended to hesitate. Finally, I said, "Deal." I felt a sense of relief when my wand was back in my sweaty hand.

Marley reappeared in the kitchen. "Maybe we should take the boys for a walk. Get rid of some of that energy."

"Good idea!" The food could wait. I needed to get over my nervous breakdown first.

Three hours later, I was sprawled on the sofa, my entire body suffering from unfamiliar aches and pains. I felt like I'd been run over by a truck that reversed and backed over me again. I'd managed to feed them and get them to bed without further incident. We skipped baths because it seemed like the safest option. Marley read them a story before retreating to the guest bedroom.

The house was quiet now. I was just about to doze off when I heard their voices outside the front door, low and angry. I debated whether to jet upstairs and pretend to be asleep in one of the beds, but I worried they'd hear my thundering footsteps. I wasn't stealthy like Alec.

"You didn't need to destroy it," Sterling said heatedly. "You're a better witch than that."

"The phone was talking to you like it was possessed," Aster said. "What choice did I have?"

"It felt passive aggressive to me," Sterling said. "You've clearly been resentful of the time I spend at the office and you took your hostility out on my phone."

"Of course I'm resentful!" she snapped. "I'm beginning to think I have something, or someone, to worry about."

"Don't be ridiculous," he replied. "The Aster I know would never doubt me, or herself. She has far more confidence than that. Frankly, darling, it's an unattractive quality I didn't realize you were capable of."

"I'll show you unattractive," she said, her voice threatening.

"Put the wand away," he warned. "We don't use magic against each other. We swore that in our wedding vows."

"We swore a lot of things in our wedding vows," she seethed. "Are you upholding them all?"

"Enough," Sterling demanded. "This conversation is beneath you."

The door opened and I pulled a decorative pillow over

my head, as though that would somehow indicate my ears weren't working.

The moment they stepped across the threshold, the argument stopped.

"How did it go?" Aster asked me, blinding me with a flash of her perfect teeth.

I yawned in an effort to appear sleepily incoherent. "Hmm? Oh, you're back. Everything was good. The boys are snoozing away and Marley is in the guest bed."

"I'll wake her, if you like." Sterling bounded up the stairs before I could object. He seemed eager to put distance between him and his wife.

I swung my legs over the side of the sofa. "Nice dinner?"

Aster's expression clouded over. "It was, until his phone started acted up. It began talking to him during the first course, chastising him for the flirtatious tone of his texts to his female co-workers. He tried to turn it off, but it wouldn't stop." Aster covered her face with her hands. "The phone began reading some of the texts out loud. It was awful. I had to do a spell to make it stop. Half the restaurant was listening. To top it off, Sterling is angry with me for destroying his phone, like I did it on purpose."

Once again, I'd managed to cause more problems than I solved. When would I learn to only use magic when I was confident of the outcome?

"Maybe you should be angry with him for sexting with other women," I said. "That seems more egregious than accidentally breaking his phone."

The sound of footsteps alerted us to Marley's presence. She rubbed her eyes and gave Aster a sleepy smile.

"The boys are sweet, but a lot of work," Marley said. "You're a good mom."

Tears welled in Aster's eyes. "Thank you, Marley. That means a lot."

I observed my cousin for a moment, uncertain how to respond to the tears. Aster wasn't much of a hugger and neither was I. What was the appropriate next step in this conversation?

"Sterling said to tell you goodnight and that he's going to bed," Marley reported.

The tears dissipated as Aster's jaw tightened. "Thank you."

"I'll meet you in the car, Marley," I said. "I need to grab a few things."

Marley was too tired to see through my ruse. "Okay," she mumbled. "'Night, Aster."

"Goodnight, sweetness," Aster replied. Once Marley departed, she looked at me. "Can I help you find something?"

I retrieved my handbag from behind the sofa. "Got it." I paused. "Aster, I have something to confess. I did a spell on Sterling's phone. I was trying to disable it temporarily, but I think I ended up creating a totem."

Aster barked a short laugh. "You put a spirit in his phone?"

I shrugged. "I was in a rush and I did the next spell that came to mind. I'm sorry it backfired."

Aster dropped onto the sofa, looking defeated. "Why did you try to disable it?"

I sat beside her. "Because I noticed how distracted he's been and I wanted the two of you to have a chance to focus solely on each other."

Aster patted my hand. "You don't need to worry about us, Ember. All marriages have their ups and downs. Sterling and I are the only ones responsible for the state of our marriage."

"He doesn't seem to be taking your concerns seriously," I said.

"It's his way," Aster said. "He's a stubborn wizard and his

immediate impulse is to push back. Once he calms down, he'll realize that his response was misguided."

"You sound confident," I said.

Aster squared her shoulders. "I have to. I have two little lives hanging in the balance." She inclined her head. "Is this because of Karl? Do you feel like Sterling and I are squandering our time together?"

I considered the question. "Maybe that's part of it, but Karl and I were so young when we got married. Too young. I suspect we would've become different people in the long run." The couple that fails to change together inevitably grows apart.

"Indeed. You became an entirely different person," Aster pointed out. "A witch, in fact."

I smiled. "Sometimes I wonder what Karl would think of all this. I bet he would think it's pretty cool. He'd definitely want Marley to inherit the magic genes."

"Sterling used to be more focused on his family," Aster said in a hushed tone. "I don't know why he's checked out."

"You're not going to address it?" I queried. "It's been going on for a while."

Aster plucked an imaginary thread from the cushion. "I don't want to rock the broomstick. We live a comfortable life. The boys are happy and thriving. I'm not willing to jeopardize any of that."

"And you think by remaining quiet that you're not already jeopardizing that?"

Aster tensed. "It's the way Mother would handle it."

"Is it?" I wasn't convinced. Aunt Hyacinth was more of a 'scorched earth' kind of witch, from what I could tell.

"Mother dislikes mess," Aster said. "She'll be appalled when she hears about the restaurant incident."

"I think she'll be more appalled to hear about Sterling's behavior," I said. "If I were him, I'd be very worried."

A smile played upon her lips. "He is deathly afraid of Mother, although he'll never admit it."

"Maybe you should remind him exactly how vengeful she can be," I suggested. "I mean, Wyatt should be example enough."

Aster balled her fists. "That werewolf was bad news from the start. Sterling is nothing like Wyatt."

I sighed. "Then I think it's high time he proves it."

CHAPTER 14

"I'm not riding a damn horse, Rose," the sheriff said. "I'm a wolf. I'd be an embarrassment to the pack."

We stood outside Rose Cottage, preparing to attend a meeting of the Council of Elders. If anyone could provide information on forgotten treasure maps, it would be the older members of Starry Hollow society. My aunt was kind enough to arrange it for us, mainly because she wanted Simon's full attention back.

"Then you'll need to shift to keep up," I said. "It's too tricky on foot and impossible by car."

"I'm happy to shift," he said. "As long as it doesn't bother you."

Did it? No, I didn't think so. I'd seen him in full wolf mode back when he was infected with a parasite, and I'd been more scared of losing him than *of* him.

"Will you frighten the horse, though?" I wasn't a competent enough rider to gain control of a spooked mount.

The sheriff stroked his chin. "Hmm. There's a good bet I would."

I remembered the new addition to the stables. "What about a unicorn?"

The sheriff's brow lifted. "You got yourself a unicorn, Rose? To the manor born, eh?"

I folded my arms in a huff. "I did not get myself anything. Aunt Hyacinth bought her for Marley, but she responds to me."

"You do have a way with animals," the sheriff said. "And I include myself in that group."

"Apparently, I inherited that 'way' from my mother," I said. "Kelsey from Kelsey's Stables knew my mother. When Marley goes riding there with Firefly, I get to talk to Kelsey about my mom. A win-win."

"Well, let's go meet this Firefly," the sheriff said. "Wouldn't want to be late for the old folks."

"The elders," I corrected him.

"That makes them sound wiser than they are. Just because they manage to dodge death longer than most doesn't make them smart. Makes them lucky."

My laugh came out more like a grunt. "I never knew you had an irreverent side to you, Sheriff."

"Seems to me you still have a lot to learn, Rose." He cocked an eyebrow. "You gonna wear that silver cloak?"

I fidgeted with my long sleeves. "It's sort of a requirement when I go to see them. A sign of respect."

"Hides your figure."

"I'm not there to get a date," I shot back.

He winked. "You never know with you, Rose."

We crossed the grounds together and the sheriff waited outside of the stables while I prepared Firefly, including a change of clothes for the sheriff once he'd shifted back to human form.

"Am I missing anything important?" I asked the unicorn.

She nudged her snout toward a heavy blanket folded on a nearby stool.

"Good thinking." There was no saddle, so I tossed the blanket over her back. I used a step stool to mount her, so I didn't make a fool of myself in front of the sheriff. I did that often enough.

"I'll follow your lead," the sheriff said, as we exited the stables.

"That'll be a new trick."

Thankfully, I remembered the way to the hidden cave and was able to steer Firefly through the forest and along the coastline. The moon remained behind the clouds, so the only light to guide us was the glow of Firefly's horn. Although I couldn't see the sheriff's wolf form, I felt his presence nearby. He managed to move in complete silence, which was both impressive and a little scary.

My aunt met us in the neck of the cave once the sheriff had made himself presentable.

"Welcome to our humble quarters," she said. "I see you put your daughter's gift to good use."

"Firefly seemed the best option with a wolf on my heels," I said.

"A reasonable assumption." Aunt Hyacinth glanced at the sheriff. "Keep your questions on point and straightforward. The council doesn't want to feel like it's being interrogated."

"No one here is a suspect," the sheriff said. "We're only trying to gather background information."

"Excellent." My aunt gave him a pointed look. "And you would be wise to curb your usual attitude."

"Attitude? I'm not Wyatt," he protested.

"No," my aunt replied. "If you were, you wouldn't be permitted here in the first place."

We traveled to the part of the cave large enough to house

the council's round table. Candlelight flickered all around us. There were two empty seats together, so we took the hint.

"Thank you for allowing me entry," Sheriff Nash said. "I've always wondered what these meetings were like."

"The location and proceedings are to be kept confidential," Victorine, the head of the vampire coven, said. "We don't care who you are." Victorine Del Bianco was nearly as formidable as Aunt Hyacinth. The sharp fangs helped.

"There was disagreement as to whether you should have been brought here unconscious," Mervin O'Malley said. The leprechaun rubbed his freckled forehead. He looked like he was still nursing a hangover.

"Duly noted," the sheriff said. Although he had an ego, he was wise enough not to give the esteemed members of the council a witty retort.

"No worries, my boy." Arthur Rutledge gave him a kind smile. "I vehemently objected to any such measures." The elderly werewolf tilted his head toward Misty Brookline, the fairy representative. "You're the sheriff of this town and that is deserving of our respect, elders or not."

"Hyacinth says you are here to ask about treasure," Oliver Dagwood interjected. "Such folly."

The sheriff shifted his focus to the elderly wizard. "We're not actually hunting for treasure. We're trying to find out more about a missing map in the hope that it will lead us to a murderer."

"It's not good for the town's reputation to have a killer on the loose," I said. "The victim was from out of town, attending a conference. If word gets out, it could hurt tourism."

"Then perhaps the local paper would be wise to suppress the story until we have answers," Victorine said. Her cool gaze rested on my aunt, the owner and operator of *Vox Populi*.

Although her expression remained serene, I could sense my aunt seething. She didn't want to be told what to do by anyone, least of all a vampire.

"No need to suppress a story that is incomplete," my aunt replied smoothly. Take that, Victorine! "Once the full story is known, the paper has a duty to report it, of course."

Amaryllis Elderflower coughed delicately. "What kind of information do you need?"

I produced the town map that Laura had marked up. "Someone who'd seen the map identified some places she thought were on it. She remembers two crossed daggers dripping with blood on the original map. Of course, this is a modern map of the town and we're not sure which spots the X's are meant to mark."

Amaryllis studied the map first. "This X is close to Casper's Revenge. That's the only place that would've been standing at a time when vampire pirates were roaming about."

"Casper's Revenge?" I echoed.

"An inn run by ghosts," Melvin interjected.

The sheriff and I exchanged looks, recognizing the name. Jeeves had mentioned the inn during our interview.

"I can't think of what this place might be," Oliver said, tapping another X. "I picture an empty lot there."

Victorine scraped her freakishly long fingernails along the table. "Have you been to the Whitethorn?"

"Not yet," the sheriff replied. "Why?"

Laura hadn't marked the Whitethorn on the map. It would have been one of the few locations I'd have recognized without help.

"Do you think the treasure's connected to Captain Black-fang?" I asked.

"I don't know the details," Victorine said. "But I've heard rumors of a treasure hidden by his first mate. Valuables secured without their fearsome leader. Since I don't recognize the symbol of crossed daggers, it's possible your map refers to that particular treasure. It would be one of the lesser known ones."

"Who would be crazy enough to go behind Captain Blackfang's back?" I asked. Someone with a death wish.

"Speak to Duncan," Victorine said. "Although I've been around for quite some time, talk of treasure and pirate lore has never held much interest for me. I simply tune it out whenever the subject is broached."

Talking to Duncan made a lot of sense. So much so, that I was annoyed I hadn't thought of it myself.

"And how are your studies progressing, Miss Rose?" Misty asked. "We understand you're in the process of training for your broomstick license."

"I am," I said. "Turns out, Florian is a good teacher."

"Florian seems to be coming into his own, as of late," Amaryllis said. "You should be proud, Hyacinth."

"I've always been proud of my children," my aunt responded crisply. She clearly disliked the implication that Florian only recently deserved praise.

"While we're on the subject, you should be proud of Deputy Bolan," the sheriff told Mervin. "He's a fantastic right hand."

"I'm sure he is, when he's allowed to do his job," Mervin blurted.

The sheriff straightened. "What's that supposed to mean?"

My stomach sank. I knew exactly what it was supposed to mean. "He's talking about me."

The sheriff clenched his teeth. "Miss Rose in no way interferes with Deputy Bolan's job."

"Then why is she here with you tonight instead of him?" Mervin asked. "It seems to me your deputy should be part of the investigation."

"He is," the sheriff insisted. "And I'll thank you not to presume to tell me how to conduct police business."

"Ember is the one who suggested speaking to us," my aunt said. "She saw the value of our collective knowledge. Your leprechaun drew no such conclusion."

Mervin's cheeks reddened. "In that case, neither did our sheriff."

A low growl came from the direction of Arthur Rutledge. "I propose we end this line of discussion before it gets ugly."

"Agreed," Misty said. "If you have an issue with the way the sheriff handles investigations, there are proper channels to go through."

Mervin backed down. "That won't be necessary. The deputy would be mortified if he knew I'd even mentioned it. He has the utmost respect for Sheriff Nash."

"As he should," Arthur grumbled.

The sheriff drew himself to his full height. "Rose, I think we're done here."

"Thank you for your help," I said. It couldn't hurt to be polite. A little something I learned from Marley.

"Good luck," Aunt Hyacinth said. "The sooner you catch the murderer, the better for us all."

The sheriff and I went straight from the council meeting to the Whitethorn. After midnight was the perfect time to speak to Duncan without too many patrons listening in. I hitched Firefly to a post outside and we sauntered into the pub like two Wild West cowboys.

"Two crossed daggers dripping with blood? I know about that map," Duncan said, once we explained the reason for our visit. "Had a bachelor party come through here about a year back looking for it as part of a scavenger hunt."

"How did they even know about its existence?" I asked.

"Word gets around when there's treasure involved," Duncan said. "The groom and best man were local. They'd probably heard the stories from when they were babes in arms."

"The pack stories don't include many vampire pirates," the sheriff said.

"No surprise there," I replied. There was no love lost between werewolves and vampires. "Have you had anyone in here recently asking about the map or treasure?"

Duncan glanced over his shoulder at his parrot, Bittersteel. "Anyone lately?"

"Not that I recall," the parrot squawked. "Maybe a snack would jog my memory."

The sheriff tapped the star on his shirt. "Maybe this bright star will jog your memory."

"Nope, no one's been asking," Bittersteel replied.

Duncan wiped a glass with a cloth. "Probably because the treasure isn't Blackfang's. Everyone associates the pub with him."

"Victorine said the treasure may have belonged to his first mate," I said.

"Irina the Bloodless," Bittersteel squawked with a passionate sigh. "Now there was a woman."

"An undead woman," Duncan corrected him.

Bittersteel seemed unperturbed. "You never saw skin so translucent."

Duncan poured a pint of ale and slid it across the bar to the lone awaiting patron. "Because she was a vampire that traveled under the cover of darkness. Her skin didn't see the sun again once she was turned, not back then."

"Were the crossed daggers her symbol?" the sheriff asked.

"Aye," Duncan said. "Dripping with the blood of her victims."

"Based on what I've heard about Blackfang, I'm surprised

he didn't steal the treasure from her before she could bury it," I said.

"She had good reason," Duncan replied.

"Why? Because she was smart enough not to trust him?" I asked.

"She learned the hard way," Duncan said. "She didn't trust him because he'd double-crossed her one too many times. In life and in love."

"They were romantically involved?" the sheriff queried.

Bittersteel squawked. "Blackfang was the luckiest vampire pirate on the planet."

"It's a shame you're not a parrot shifter," I said. "You'd have a better chance at snagging one of these ladies you admire so much."

"I have other good qualities," Bittersteel said. "They don't call me Big Bird for nothin'."

"No one calls you Big Bird except maybe the sparrows," Duncan admonished him.

I stifled a giggle. "Tell me more about Irina." Maybe there would be clues in her story that could help us now.

Duncan poured me another drink. "Her fiery red hair matched her temper. She was as ruthless and passionate as her captain."

"Probably why they had that push-pull relationship," I said. They were like magnets, attracting and repelling each other in equal measure.

"Irina acquired the treasure while Blackfang was off with one of his wenches," Duncan continued. "Of course, Irina didn't know this at the time. She planned to make the treasure a gift to him."

I took a long drink and felt the liquid warm my stomach. "But that didn't happen?"

"When she arrived back in Starry Hollow with a full crew and the treasure, she was riding high," Duncan said.

"Until she located her beloved captain in a compromising position."

"It wasn't your mother, was it?" I asked in a hushed tone.

"No, thank the devil," Duncan said. "Irina would've skinned her alive. It was a barmaid from here, actually. Young Lucy Clover."

"That's another connection to the Whitethorn," I said. All pirate roads seemed to lead to the ancient pub.

"Irina discovered their tryst here," Duncan continued. "The vicious vampire attacked Lucy, not realizing that Lucy was a powerful witch."

"One of ours?" I queried.

Duncan nodded solemnly. "They fought, and Irina was scarred by fire. Lucy was an accomplished elemental witch, it turned out."

"All this over an undead pirate?" I scoffed. "He hardly seems worth the trouble."

"Irina was madly in love with him," Duncan said. "She would have moved mountains to get that treasure for him. She was devastated to return and find him with someone else."

"Irina should have attacked Blackfang, not Lucy," I said.

"Oh, she did, too," Duncan said. "It didn't end well for either of them. Irina eventually succumbed to her injuries without revealing the location of the treasure to Blackfang, but she supposedly managed to hide clues to the treasure before she died."

"And a map was born," the sheriff said.

I finished my drink and my head swam with emotions. I felt sorry for Irina. To literally go to the ends of the earth for the man she loved, only to be betrayed...It was heartbreaking. Then again, she had to know what kind of vampire she was in love with. Blackfang had a reputation and the two of them had certainly traveled together long enough for Irina to have witnessed his behavior firsthand.

"Love makes paranormals do crazy things," the sheriff said, as though reading my thoughts.

It certainly did. "Have you ever searched for her treasure?" I asked. "Maybe she hid it here to make a statement."

"'Course," Duncan said. "Nights when I get bored or lonely. Or a visitor reminds me about it. I had one werewolf in here trying to sniff its location. That kickstarted my search again."

"Don't forget the psychic," Bittersteel interjected.

Duncan chuckled. "A two-bit con artist, that one was. Seems unnecessary when you can find a perfectly good psychic over on Seers Row."

I blinked. "Seers Row?"

Duncan seemed surprised. "You haven't been there yet? It's on the street by the Pointy Hat. A psychic in every building. Clarissa the Clairvoyant, Frida the Future. At least a dozen."

"All authentic?" I asked.

"Absolutely," he replied. "They take great pride in their work."

"Are they like Artemis Haverford?" I asked. "Do they use tea leaves and runes?"

Duncan rubbed his beard. "I reckon they use a variety of methods, depending on the type of paranormal. Witches might use runes, but an angel wouldn't."

I gulped. "An angel psychic?"

"Sure," Duncan said. "I can't believe you haven't come across one yet."

"With white wings and everything?" I couldn't quite believe it.

"Some of them use magic to hide their wings, more for convenience than anything else. Angel wings are much bigger and wider than fairy and pixie wings. Damn annoying in the grocery store when you're trying to get around one with your cart."

"Like Rick," I said. "He's the minotaur who co-owns Paradise Found. He shifts into human form to make life easier."

Recognition flickered in Duncan's eyes. "I know 'im. Nice fella. Puts away ale like nobody I've ever seen, including your brother, Sheriff." Duncan peered at me. "Now that you mention it, I hear that minotaur's dating one of your fancy cousins. Is that true?"

Crap on a stick. Talk about a gossip mill. "They're friends. That's all I'm willing to say." Until Aunt Hyacinth knew anything, I was keeping a lid on it. Although if word was getting around, Linnea needed to pick up the pace. I didn't want to be a fly on the wall for that conversation.

Okay, truthfully, I kinda did.

"Thanks for your help, Duncan," the sheriff said.

"Happy to serve," Duncan replied. "Ale, information, whatever's required."

"A lot of residents seem to think the treasure talk is nonsense," I said. "But the stories seem to ring true."

"Oh, they're as true as my fangs," Duncan said, flicking one of them. "Just because no one's found the treasure doesn't mean it isn't here. Just means Irina did a good job of hiding it from Blackfang."

So Irina got her revenge in the end, by denying her lover the one thing he valued most—stolen treasure.

CHAPTER 15

THE NEXT MORNING, Sheriff Nash and I stood outside of a place called Bewitching Bites. It was the one location marked on Laura's map that no one seemed able to identify, which was surprising since the building was impossible to miss. It resembled a life-size gingerbread house, complete with downspouts made of icing and gumdrops covering the roof.

"I can't believe you've never been in here before," I said. "If I'd known it was here, Marley and I would have spent every weekend stocking up on supplies."

"They're not supplies, Rose," the sheriff said.

"Maybe not to you." I pushed open the door and walked beneath the arched candy canes to the interior of the shop. The display cases ran the width of the shop and I went straight over to admire the colorful assortment of sweets.

"I can't say that I mind a candy store on the treasure map," I said, scanning the array of confectionery options.

"Me neither," the sheriff said. He bent down to examine the bottom row of sweets.

"I didn't realize you had a sweet tooth," I said.

"I like a good bite of chocolate just as much as the next

165

werewolf." He pointed to a dark chocolate witch's hat. "Now that's clever."

"This whole place is clever," I said. I looked upward to admire the shimmering sugar plum candies strung along the ceiling like fairy lights.

"What a lovely compliment," a female voice rang out. The woman emerged from a backroom with a tray of small chocolate cauldrons filled with tiny pieces of candy. She wore a plain smock and her brown hair was pulled back in a tight bun. "We take great pride in our work. Bewitching Bites has been family owned and operated for two hundred years." She beamed at us. "I'm Hedy Gerstberger. I run this place with my daughter, Hannah."

"Two hundred years? I guess that explains why they're on the map," the sheriff whispered.

"I bet this shop has a fascinating history," I said to Hedy.

"Oh, yes, indeed." She slid the tray of cauldrons into an empty section of the display case. "We've been the confectioner of choice for all kinds of famous paranormals. Political leaders, generals, royals, pirates. You name it, we probably made chocolate for it."

"Pirates, did you say?" I queried.

Hedy nodded vigorously. "Not just any pirates. Vampire pirates, the most feared kind on the high seas."

"I don't know why it surprises me that vampire pirates would enjoy a good chocolate pretzel every now and again, but it does," I said.

Hedy closed the display case door. "My family kept a detailed log of purchases by their more esteemed clientele. Captain Blackfang preferred chocolate-covered cherries. His first mate liked chocolate and coconut."

"Amazing," I said. "Did the pirates pay with doubloons?"

"They paid with good coin from around the world, which is one of the reasons my family was happy to serve them,"

Hedy said. "I believe the most extravagant item they received was a small carving of a solid gold minotaur."

The sheriff whistled. "That'd be worth millions."

"It would," Hedy agreed, "which is why it's so distressing that we have no further record of it."

"You had it listed as a payment, but you don't know what happened to it?" I queried.

Hedy nodded. "It's on the ledger as payment received, but, sadly, the trail ends there."

"No family stories as to what might have become of it?" the sheriff asked. "I bet that's the kind of tale that gets passed down from generation to generation."

Hedy gave a dismissive wave. "Oh, there are plenty of stories. Not sure I believe any of 'em."

"You never followed up on any of them?" I asked. "Tried to track down the minotaur?"

Hedy scrutinized me. "Are you here to buy chocolate?"

"Um, I'm salivating over your chocolate toads with a gooey caramel center," I said. "So, yes, I am."

The sheriff grimaced. "Toads, Rose?"

"You don't have to try one," I said. "Choose your own."

The sheriff continued to review the offerings. "What are those covered in?" He tapped the glass in front of shiny golden apples.

"Not actual gold, if that's what you're worried about," Hedy said. "We use an old fairy recipe that makes a sweetener look like melted gold."

The sheriff clicked his teeth. "Good to know. I have a pretty sharp set of chompers, but I wouldn't be attempting to eat melted gold with them."

"Would you like to try one?" Hedy offered. "Free sample for the sheriff."

"I wouldn't want to bite into a whole apple in case I don't want to finish it," the sheriff said.

"Never fear," Hedy said, retrieving a miniature golden apple from an undisclosed source. "We have samples in smaller sizes for that very reason."

Sheriff Nash popped the tiny treat into his mouth and chewed. "Delicious."

Hedy seemed delighted. "Wonderful. Anything else you'd like to try?"

"Would it be possible to look at some of the old records," I said. "I'm writing a paper for my history class about local legends and I'd love to include information about the missing minotaur. My teacher would get a kick out of it." I paused, thinking of my owl shifter professor. "Or a hoot."

"I don't know," Hedy said. "Those records are confidential."

I glanced at the sheriff, not sure whether he'd want to make the request official. He ignored my lead. Instead, he carried on studying the contents of the case.

"Sheriff?" I prompted.

"What? I can't decide. Maybe one of those sugar plum fairy wands. I like how they sparkle." He seemed to forget why we were there.

Hedy retrieved one from the case. "These are one of my favorites." She waved it in the air. "I love how it catches the light."

The sheriff stared at it like he was a cat following a laser. "So pretty," he agreed.

"Sheriff?" I queried. He gobbled down the wand and turned his attention straight back to the case. I tried again. "Granger?"

"You can have something, too, Rose," he said. "I won't deprive you. It's not like you need to watch your weight."

"Gee, thanks," I said. "My weight's not really the problem."

He stood and blinked at me. "There's a problem? Don't deny it. I can tell from your tone that there is." He grinned at

Hedy. "She skips over passive and goes right to aggressive." He lowered his voice. "That's because she's from New Jersey."

"It's not a secret," I said. "You don't need to whisper."

"You should try a sample," Hedy said, holding out one of the toads I'd been eyeing. "I insist."

She shouldn't have added that last part. If she hadn't said 'I insist,' I probably would've eaten it. As it happened, my natural tendency was to object when someone 'insisted.' So I did.

"No, thanks," I said.

Hedy clenched her jaw. "How about a nice white chocolate rabbit in a hat?"

"Don't think so," I said. "I've lost my taste for sweets today. Maybe another time."

Hedy wasn't accepting no for an answer. "No one leaves Bewitching Bites without trying a sample. It's unheard of."

The more she pushed, the more suspicious I became.

"This one," the sheriff said, pointing to a chocolate dwarf hat filled with colorful candies made to look like gemstones from the mines.

"I don't have any miniatures of those," Hedy said. "Would you like a whole one?"

"Yes," the sheriff said.

I moved between the sheriff and the display case. "No, he will not have one. He's had enough, thank you."

"Rose, what's the matter?" he asked. "I thought you were excited to be here. Nothing like this back in Maple Shade, is there?"

"Not quite." Although we had our share of street corner drug dealers. "We need to go, Sheriff. We have that appointment."

I grabbed him by the shoulders and attempted to steer him to the exit. A younger woman appeared in front of us, blocking our path.

"She hasn't had a sample, Mother?" the young woman asked.

"No, Hannah," Hedy replied. "Only the sheriff."

"You might want to say that again," I said. "Sheriff. When he finds out what you've done, he'll arrest you."

"What have we done?" Hedy asked. "He's enjoyed a bit of candy and then he'll be on his way. No harm done."

I whirled around and stared at her. "What are you hiding? Why do you want us to forget why we came and leave?"

Hedy seemed surprised by my astute assessment. "I don't know what you mean."

"It's the gold minotaur, isn't it?" I asked. "You're hiding something."

"Mother?" Hannah's voice was unsteady.

I faced the young woman blocking the door. She was shorter and thinner than me. I could probably take her if I had to. I didn't know what kind of magic the mother and daughter duo possessed, however. That gave me pause.

Hedy tossed her daughter one of the sample golden apples. "Make her eat this."

Hannah caught the sample in her hands, her eyes never leaving mine. "With pleasure."

"Not gonna happen, Hannah," I said. "If my own father couldn't persuade me to eat brussel sprouts, you certainly can't force me to eat whatever magical candy you've got there."

"It's only magical because it tastes delicious," Hannah lied.

"It really is delicious, Rose," the sheriff said. "Try one. Don't be shy." He laughed. "What am I saying? You don't know the meaning of the word 'shy.'"

"You're both going to regret this," I said.

"No, we won't," Hannah said. "The sheriff won't remember a thing about his visit after he leaves." She held up the sample apple. "And neither will you."

I racked my brain to come up with a spell on the fly. I'd made so many mistakes lately. What if I screwed up and hurt the sheriff in the process? I couldn't risk it, not after what I'd done to Alec. And the innocent meatloaf, of course.

On the other hand, these two women were hiding information that we clearly needed. If there was a chance it was connected to the murder, I had to know.

"Fine, I'll eat it," I said. "Hand it over." As she extended her arm, I pretended to look up in surprise. "Oh, no!"

As I hoped, both women looked up, distracted. It was long enough. I whipped out my wand.

"*Consto!*" I said.

"What are you doing, Rose?" the sheriff asked.

"I think they should enjoy their sweets as much as others do," I said.

The Gerstbergers remained frozen in position as I stuck a tiny sample apple in both of their mouths. I aimed my wand at each of them and then said, "*Mando.*" Chew. I didn't want them to choke to death.

Once they'd swallowed, I unfroze the women. Hannah smiled at us.

"We hope you enjoyed your visit," she said pleasantly. "Come back soon."

"Thanks, we will," I said, grabbing the sheriff by the arm and pulling him out the door. I didn't ever want to go back, but we had to, now that we knew they were hiding something. Maybe it was only a family recipe for the best chocolate in the paranormal world, but the jaded part of me worried that it was something far more sinister.

I wasn't thrilled to show up on the doorstep of Casper's Revenge by myself, but the sheriff and deputy were called to a meeting with Tish and Belvedere for an update on the case.

Since the sheriff and I had both let this place slip through the cracks, I thought it was time to pay a visit and cross it off the list.

I'd never believed in ghosts. My father avoided such topics, probably because he feared saying too much and revealing a sliver of his past. Our past. He was very particular about the wisdom he imparted and the anecdotes he shared. Ghosts didn't make the cut. So far, the only ghost I'd 'met' was Jefferson, the manservant at Haverford House.

I shivered before I even took hold of the brass knocker. It was the head of a minotaur, nostrils flaring, which would have intimidated me if I hadn't already met Rick.

"Hey there, big guy," I said softly, and banged the brass hoop of his nose against the door. The door creaked open and I gulped down as much air as I could manage before stepping inside.

"Hello?" I called. The foyer was devoid of paranormals, ghosts included. It was an attractive space, with portraits on the wall and a crackling fireplace. I wasn't sure why the fireplace was on when the weather in Starry Hollow was a balmy seventy degrees.

"Because the house has a constant chill," a disembodied voice said. "It's like living in an icebox."

I whirled around in search of the source. "Who said that?"

"Fire warms us from the inside out," a second, more soothing voice said. "Our guest knows fire, don't you, dear? You've commanded it."

"No," I said slowly. "I used rain to put out a fire." The ghost seemed to be referencing my crisis with Jimmy the Lighter.

"She could command it if she wanted to," the first voice said. "She has a streak of elemental power. I sense it."

"Who cares about power? It's sympathy this girl is in dire need of," another voice said. "Send her to my room."

"No," the first voice objected. "I distinctly feel her need for tough love. She belongs in my room."

I felt an unseen hand push me toward the staircase. I rallied my courage. "Hold up there, eager apparitional beavers. I'm not going to anybody's room. I'm here to ask questions."

"I love your shoes," the third voice said. "If I were still alive, I would absolutely wear those with my black mini-dress."

"You never wore a mini-dress," the first voice argued. "Not with those varicose veins you had."

"Nobody would notice the veins with those shoes," the softer voice replied. "I'd be like Dorothy in her ruby red slippers. She couldn't go anywhere without someone noticing them."

"That was because they belonged to the Wicked Witch of the East," the first voice grumbled. "You've completely misunderstood the point of the shoes."

"Um, excuse me?" I interrupted. "I'd like to ask a few questions if you have time between pointless arguments."

"Ooh, a smartass," the second voice said. "How delightful."

"We'll answer your questions," the third voice said, "but first you need to be an official guest."

"But I don't want to stay," I said. "I live locally."

"No matter," the second voice said. "Rules are rules."

I huffed. "Fine. How do I become an official guest?"

"There's a registry over there on the table," the first voice said. "Add your name and address."

"And positive comments about your stay are also welcome," the third voice said.

"But I'm not…" I stopped. There was no point in correcting her. Instead, I headed to the table and added my name and address to the registry. In the comments section, I wrote, "TBD."

"Interesting choice. It's like a threat," the second voice said.

"She's grown on me significantly since she arrived," the first voice said. "Initially, I was put off by the hair."

"Hey!" I objected. "What's wrong with my hair?" I held up a hand. "Wait, don't answer that."

"We have all the amenities you need, dear," the second voice said. "A flatiron, perhaps? There are several rooms to choose from and a hot tub on the back porch. The bathtubs are all claw foot."

"I won't be needing a tub," I said. "Hot or otherwise."

"Oh, but it's a must," the second voice said. "It's part of being a guest here."

"She needs a spot of tea," the third voice said. "I'll take care of it."

"My name is Ember," I said, as I felt a burst of air push me toward the room on the left. "I'm investigating a murder."

"A murder? How exciting!" the second voice said.

"Not for the victim," the first voice said.

"Would you mind telling me your names?" I asked. "I'd like to think of you as more than voices in the air." And it might calm my nerves.

"I'm Ethel," the second voice said. "The grumpy one is Allan, and the one preparing your tea is Irma."

"Are there only three of you?" I asked.

"No, but we're the three in charge today," Ethel said. "We rotate."

I entered the next room. The sign above me read 'Parlor Room' in fancy script lettering. A chair slid out from under the small, oval table and I sat.

"Is this place really operated entirely by ghosts?" I queried.

"That's right," Allan said. "We're a special type of inn."

"Because you're all ghosts?"

"And because we cater to our guests' emotional needs," Allan said.

"Well, some of us do," Ethel said pointedly.

"Tough love fulfills an emotional need," Allan shot back. "Just because you don't agree with it, doesn't mean it's untrue."

A silver tray floated down in front of me. It carried a teapot, teacup, a sugar bowl, and a small milk jug. When I reached for the pot, one of the unseen hands smacked me.

"Ouch!" I said.

"We cater to *you*," Irma said.

"Okay, no need for violence." My hands moved to my sides. I watched as the tea was poured and then the sugar and milk added.

"Not too much milk," I said. "I like it strong."

"I know, dear," Irma said. "I read your preferences the moment you walked in."

"That's...creepy," I said.

"Don't let it sit or it will get cold," Ethel said.

"She doesn't want to burn her tongue, Ethel," Allan snapped.

I held up my hands. "I'm a grown woman. I can decide for myself whether the tea is the right temperature."

"She is quite grown, isn't she?" Irma said. "Breastfeeding was good to you, wasn't it? So fortunate."

"Yes, those boobs are the ideal size," Ethel said. "What are they? A 36C?"

I wrapped my cardigan around my T-shirt. "That's personal."

"They're a bit lopsided," Allan grumbled.

"Seriously?" I objected hotly. "It isn't really polite to critique someone's body without their consent."

"We're only trying to cheer you up," Ethel said. "We can tell you've been unhappy lately."

"We excel at compliments!" Irma added.

"I don't," Allan said.

I sipped my tea. "I haven't been unhappy."

"No?" Irma queried. "How odd. You radiate sadness and loss."

"I told you she just needs tough love," Allan said. "Send her to my room."

I set down my teacup. "I'm not going to anyone's room until you explain what you mean."

"Like Allan said, the inn caters to its guests emotional needs," Ethel said. "If someone arrives in need of tough love, they go to Allan's room and he provides the emotional support they need. If the visitor needs cheering…"

"They steer clear of Allan. Got it," I said.

"Guests tell us their problems," Ethel explained. "Even if we can't fix their problems, they feel better having discussed the matter with someone else."

"So you're kind of like a confessional in a church?" I asked.

"We're a bit more interactive," Irma replied. "We don't drop rosary beads from the ceiling and tell them to pray. We offer guidance and support."

"Some people find comfort in rosary beads and prayer," I said.

"*People* don't come here," Allan said. "Paranormals do."

Fair enough.

"Well, I'm sorry to break the news, but I'm not here for guidance, or support, or rosary beads, for that matter. I need to talk about a treasure map."

"Ooh, which one?" Ethel asked. "I do love a good story."

"I don't know which one," I said. "But your inn was mentioned by the man in possession of the map the night before he died and it's marked on the map." A breeze tickled the back of my neck as a ghost drifted past.

"Really?" Irma asked. "Are we supposed to have buried treasure somewhere?"

"I don't know," I said. "I'm only following a lead. Has anyone else been here asking questions?"

"No, in fact things have been oddly quiet, haven't they, Irma?" Ethel asked.

"Very much so," Irma said. "I've been bored senseless."

"I associate the Whitethorn, or some other pub, with vampire pirate treasure," Allan said. "Captain Blackfang never would've set foot in here, not with our special brand of hospitality."

I sipped my tea, noting the perfect temperature. "Yes, I know about him. This map seems to be connected to his first mate, Irina. She was in love with him, but it didn't end well."

"Great Mother of Invention," Allan hissed.

"What is it, Allan?" Ethel asked. "Did a guest leave the tap on in your bathroom again? I told you to post a reminder on the mirror."

"No, there's a strange man in the backyard, near the hydrangeas," Allan said. "He's digging with a shovel."

"What?" Ethel and Irma shrieked. The table shook and my teacup rattled. I grabbed the cup and steadied it before the tea spilled.

"Would you like me to deal with him?" I asked. "Or, I can call the sheriff."

"Call the sheriff," Allan said. "I'll deal with this monster. Imagine coming onto someone's property and mucking up their garden. Filthy animal!"

"Show him some tough love, Allan," Ethel cheered.

I shot off a quick text to the sheriff and hurried to the backyard. By the time I got there, the intruder was unconscious on the ground and tied up with a garden hose like a trussed pig.

"I need him awake so I can ask questions," I said.

A bucket of water floated over and tipped sideways, dumping the contents on him. He sputtered and bolted upright.

"Welcome back. What's your name?" I asked.

He cocked his head. "You look familiar."

"Let me take a stab in the dark," I said. "You're a butler."

His brow lifted. "How did you know?"

I reached into his shirt pocket, where the edge of the map peeked out. "Where did you get this?"

"That's mine."

"If this is yours, then that makes you a murderer," I said. "So let me ask you again, where did you get this map?" When I spotted the symbol of the crossed daggers in the bottom corner, I knew for certain it was the missing map.

"Ooh, she's good," Allan said.

"I like what you did there," Ethel agreed.

The intruder writhed on the ground, struggling to locate the source of the voices. "Who's talking?"

"They're ghosts," I said. "And they own this property that you've trespassed on." I unfolded the map the rest of the way and saw where Casper's Revenge had been marked. "You think Irina's treasure is here?"

"Who's Irina?" he asked.

"Oh, you don't even know the story," I said. "That's too bad. Tell me where you got the map because the last time it was seen was on Higgins, which doesn't bode well for you."

The intruder's eyes popped. "The dead butler?"

"That's right."

"My name's Jeremy Higginbotham," he sputtered. "I found the map at my hotel. It was stuck to the trash chute on the third floor. I went to throw away a bag on my way out and saw it."

"Why didn't you turn it in?" I asked.

"I didn't know it was connected to the murder, I swear," Higginbotham said.

"How could you not know?" I asked. "It's all anyone can talk about."

"I knew about the murder," he said. "I didn't know anything about a treasure map."

"What makes you think treasure is buried here?" I asked.

"Nothing in particular," he said. "I decided to go around and dig up everywhere on the map, see if I struck gold. I figured it would keep me busy while we were waiting on the sheriff to tell us we could leave town."

I examined the map in my hands. There were patches of dried blood on the parchment. Higgins' blood, presumably. Other than that, it wasn't as worn as I would've expected, considering its age.

"It's been in a vault for decades," I said, admiring its excellent condition. "Like Irina, it didn't see sunlight very often."

And thanks to the murderer, it nearly never saw sunlight again.

CHAPTER 16

THE APHRODITE HOTEL reminded me of a five-star hotel in the human world. While it lacked the traditional elegance of Palmetto House or the quirkiness of Casper's Revenge, its marble floors and imposing columns made it clear that it catered to a certain class of paranormal, including their butlers in Higginbotham's case.

The manager's gaze flickered to Raoul. "Pets are not permitted in this establishment."

"We're not checking in," I argued. "We just want to check out your garbage chute on the third floor."

I think the more salient point is that I'm not a pet, Raoul said. *Tell him that.*

I ignored my familiar. "We'll be five minutes."

"I don't think so," the manager said.

"Is there a problem, Rose?" Sheriff Nash appeared beside me. "I told you to wait for me to park the car."

The manager's face turned beet red. "Terribly sorry, Sheriff. I didn't realize this was part of an official investigation."

"It's okay," the sheriff said. "My friend likes to shift before the full moon, if you know what I mean."

"I do, sir." The manager glanced at Raoul. "And this animal will be under your supervision?"

The sheriff patted the raccoon's head. "Unfortunately."

Hey! Raoul objected. *I'm not a child.*

"Good luck with your investigation, Sheriff," the manager said. "The staircase to your left is the quickest way to the third floor."

"Isn't the elevator the quickest way to the third floor?" I queried.

"Not with a raccoon it isn't," the manager replied coolly.

Racist, Raoul muttered.

We climbed the stairs to the third floor and easily located the trash chute. I pulled down the handle and popped it open.

"Sheriff," I said slowly. "I see something stuck on the side of the chute."

"It could be any number of things," he replied. "How much garbage has been sent down here since the murder?"

"Not trash. I think it's dried blood," I said, squinting in the darkness. I retrieved my wand and pointed into the chute. "*Lumina.*"

The sheriff peered over my shoulder. "How about that? Looks like Higginbotham was telling the truth after all. Can you do a spell that swabs the blood from here so neither of us needs to climb inside?"

I gave him a haughty look. "On what planet would I be the one climbing inside?" I turned my focus back to the blood. "I'll see what I can do about a spell."

Raoul tugged on my shirt. *Not everything is easily solved with magic.*

"I know that," I said. "You witnessed the Great Meatloaf Explosion. Now be quiet and let me think."

He cleared his throat and continued to stare at me. Finally, I connected the dots.

"Oh," I said. "I suppose you can climb in there."

He held his paw out to the sheriff. *Evidence kit, please.*

"He needs the evidence kit," I translated.

The sheriff gaped at my raccoon familiar. "I can call Deputy Bolan. He's small enough to fit."

Raoul rolled his eyes. *Does he really think the leprechaun will thank him for that privilege? A trash chute is a raccoon's playground slide.*

I eyed him suspiciously. "You want to make a deal."

Of course I do, he replied. *I'm an opportunist. It's in my nature.*

I folded my arms and looked at the sheriff. "Raoul will do it in exchange for letting him slide down the chute and climb around in the trash receptacle."

Sheriff Nash scrunched his nose. "As long as he can get himself out again. We're not fishing him out."

Raoul waved a dismissive paw. *Child's play.* He took the evidence kit in his teeth and climbed inside.

"I thought you weren't a child," I shot back.

Once he'd scraped enough blood for the kit, he slid it back up the chute.

"Don't come back to the cottage until you've washed up," I called after him.

"The blood must be the reason it stuck to the side of the chute." Sheriff Nash sealed the evidence bag. "We'll test it for a match with Higgins."

Hey, boss lady. I'm not alone down here.

I froze. *What do you mean?* I heard Raoul grunt and groan. Sounds of a scuffle?

"What's the matter, Rose?" the sheriff asked.

I peered down the chute and saw Raoul's beady eyes glitter in the darkness. "Who's down there with you?"

My raccoon familiar's claws clicked against the metal chute as he struggled back up. *He's heavier than he looks.*

"Who?" I shouted. I cleared the way as Raoul emerged, dragging an unconscious animal behind him. He pushed the reddish brown creature onto the floor of the hotel corridor.

"You found a fox?" the sheriff asked.

Tell your boyfriend to use his nose, Raoul said.

"Why is he unconscious?" I asked.

I may have hit him over the head with a piece of plywood.

Sheriff Nash sniffed the air. "He's not an ordinary fox."

Finally, Raoul declared. *I guess it's a good thing he's attractive. Guy's gotta have something going for him.*

The sheriff nudged the fox with the toe of his boot. I watched in amazement as the fox shifted to human form. A naked man.

A familiar naked man.

"Jenkins?" I queried.

His dark eyes fluttered open. He panicked when he realized the sheriff and I were standing over him.

"What happened?" he asked.

I gestured to my familiar. "Trevor Jenkins, meet my familiar, Raoul."

Jenkins balked. "You have a trash panda as a familiar?"

The sheriff removed his jacket and tossed it to Jenkins. "Mind telling me what you were doing in there?"

"This isn't even your hotel," I said. "You're staying at Palmetto House."

Jenkins covered himself with the jacket. "Could we maybe go into a conference room or something? I'm feeling a little exposed."

Raoul scampered down the hall. *There's an empty room here.*

The sheriff helped Jenkins to his feet and we accompanied him into the room. He replaced the sheriff's jacket with one of the white, fluffy robes.

"Let me guess," the sheriff began, "you were searching for the map."

Jenkins knew he was caught. "I haven't found it, in case you're wondering."

"What makes you think it's somewhere in the trash?" the sheriff asked. "Seems like something the killer might know."

"I've been listening to the other butlers, even followed a few of them, but no one seemed to have the map," Jenkins explained. "I decided to start searching the garbage in each hotel connected to the conference attendees. I've been working my way through them all, not too difficult in my fox form. When I smelled the blood in this chute, I thought I might be on to a winner."

"Hate to break the news, but you won't find it there," the sheriff said. "We have the map."

Jenkins' expression soured. "That's unfortunate."

"Are you a werefox?" I asked.

Jenkins lowered his gaze to the floor. "I'm a kitsune."

"You're a what?" I asked. It sounded like he'd identified himself as a musical instrument.

The sheriff looked at me. "A kitsune. A werefox of Japanese descent. They're known tricksters." He shifted his attention back to Jenkins. "Or thieves, depending on their chosen path."

Jenkins folded his arms, looking ridiculous in the puffy marshmallow robe. "Yes, I'm a professional thief. That's why Mr. Stanhope hired me. He wanted me to steal the map from Higgins and find the treasure."

"I've heard of butlers going above and beyond the call of duty, but sending you to steal for him..." I shook my head.

"He is my employer, but I'm not his butler. There's a real Jenkins, but he's at the estate. Mr. Stanhope sent me in his place."

The sheriff leaned forward, his voice low. "What's your real name?"

Jenkins shrank back. "Hitachi. Ken Hitachi."

The sheriff paced the crowded room. "You're telling me that Mr. Stanhope sent you here to steal a treasure map from his dead sister's butler?"

"That's right," Hitachi said.

The sheriff fixed him with a hard stare. "And the butler ends up dead, but you had nothing to do with it?"

"I admit that I came here to steal the map from Higgins, but I didn't get the chance to make a move," Hitachi insisted. "He died before I could do anything."

"Didn't Higgins know you weren't the real Jenkins?" I asked.

Hitachi shook his head. "They never met. The estates are nowhere near each other."

"How did Mr. Stanhope know the map would even be here?" I asked.

Hitachi tightened the belt of the robe. "He originally hired me to steal the map from Lottie Stanhope's vault, but it was gone when I arrived. When Mr. Stanhope heard from relatives that Higgins was planning to attend the conference in Starry Hollow, he suspected the map would come with him."

"So your employer thinks Higgins planned to steal the treasure for himself?" I asked. It seemed to be the only explanation for Higgins to bring the map with him.

Hitachi slumped in his chair. "Maybe he saw a golden opportunity, now that Lottie Stanhope was dead. I don't know. I'm only given the barest of details, enough to get the job done." He heaved a sigh. "Which I failed to do."

"Couldn't Mr. Stanhope simply have asked his sister for the map?" I asked.

"Lottie and her father were very close, and she refused to give my employer anything connected to him. She was never interested in the treasure, but it didn't matter. When Lottie died, my employer decided this was his chance to recover the map, but everything in the home, including the contents of the vault, was left to Laura."

"And she wouldn't let him have it, either?" I asked.

Hitachi shrugged. "I'm not sure whether he even asked. He's been estranged from his sister and her family for years. When Lottie died, he hired me."

"How do we know you're telling the truth?" The sheriff asked.

"You can verify my story with Lawrence Stanhope," he said. "Although he won't be happy about it. As for the murder, you don't have any evidence that ties me to his death. I was in the room with everyone else when he staggered in."

"Every butler in the conference was in the room at the time," I said. "The timing still suggests it was one of you."

"There's something else," Hitachi said. "A scent."

The sheriff squinted at him. "What kind of scent?"

"A floral perfume. Faint now, but sickeningly sweet," Hitachi said. "I smelled it in the chute here."

Raoul nodded in agreement. *Disgusting.*

"It wasn't the first time I'd smelled it," Hitachi said.

"Let me guess," I said. "The first time you smelled it was when you went to steal the map from Lottie Stanhope's vault."

Hitachi nodded solemnly.

The sheriff's knowing gaze met mine. "This was never about the treasure."

"No," I said quietly. My thoughts turned to Irina, a vampire scorned. "It wasn't."

The sheriff released Ken Hitachi and took the evidence kit

back to the office. He made me swear not to make a move until he returned. I sent Raoul to get me a latte from the downstairs lobby.

You know they're not going to wait on a raccoon, right?

"Do your best."

Are you just trying to get rid of me so you can snoop around the suspect's room by yourself?

"Consider this a trust exercise. I ask you to do something, and you do it." Ian would be so proud.

Sounds more like a discipline exercise. He harrumphed before heading into the stairwell.

Laura Stanhope's room was just around the corner from where we spoke to Ken Hitachi. She must have returned to her hotel room straight from the convention center and chucked the bloodstained map down the trash chute, or tried to.

I told myself that I would only look around the room for evidence before the sheriff arrived. The door was ajar with a maid's cart partially blocking the entryway. Perfect timing.

I pulled the 'H' rune from my pocket and turned myself invisible. Homework for Hazel accomplished. I slipped into the hotel room, unnoticed. With the maid standing within feet of me, I had to wait until she moved into the bathroom to open and close the drawers. I was still in the middle of searching for evidence when Laura returned to the room. Oops.

"So sorry, miss," the maid said. "I'll be out of your way in just a second." She pushed her cart into the hallway and closed the door before I had a chance to follow.

Laura tossed her handbag onto the bed, her body weary. She removed a clip from her hair and let it fall loose to her shoulders. She set the clip on the dresser and sighed deeply.

"Go home, Laura," she told herself. "There's no point in staying. He's dead and you can't change that, not without an expensive necromancer, and you know that's risky business. Remember Mommy's second husband. Total disaster."

Laura's floral perfume permeated the air. In a confined space, the scent was overpowering.

"You're an absolute fool, Laura," she continued. "You should have known you'd screw this up, just like you screw everything up. He loved you, yet you refused to believe it." She dropped onto the edge of the bed. "And now he's dead because of you."

I halted. Was that a metaphorical statement, or an admission of guilt? One look at her face and I could see the truth. I saw it in her frown lines. In her downturned mouth. In her tragic gaze. Laura Stanhope killed Higgins. I needed to tell the sheriff.

"Come now, Laura," she said. "You know what you need to do. No Mommy. No Higgins. The only paranormals in the world who ever cared for you are gone." She bit her lip, fighting the emotions. I watched as she pulled several vials of potion from her handbag and set them on the dresser. "What's the point in carrying on?"

Oh no. She wouldn't drink them all, would she? Murderer or not, I couldn't let her do that.

Laura popped the lid off the first vial. "Perhaps I'll see you soon, Higgins, so that I can apologize and tell you how much I really cared."

I pulled the rune from my pocket and made myself visible again. "Laura, stop!"

She dropped the vial on the floor, spilling the contents. "What the devil?" She spun toward me. "Where did you come from?"

I didn't answer. "Please don't kill yourself. No matter what you did to him, Higgins wouldn't want that."

Laura regarded me carefully. "What do you mean?"

Hmm. Maybe I'd overplayed my hand. I decided to plow

ahead anyway. "I know you killed him. You stabbed him in the convention center restroom with the corkscrew from the Wine Cellar Room. The question is—why?"

Laura cast a sidelong glance at the remaining vials on the dresser. I could see the wheels turning, calculating whether they'd be enough to do the job without the third vial.

"Please don't," I said.

"I didn't intend to use the corkscrew," she said finally. "I only meant to threaten her with it."

"Her?" I echoed. "Who's her?"

Laura closed her eyes. "No one. The woman I imagined he was meeting."

"In the bathroom of the convention center?" I asked, perplexed.

"That's where I confronted *him*," she said. "I'd lifted the corkscrew when I toured the room earlier, thinking I'd see them together before registration, sipping coffee together. Contemplating their new life. But he was alone. Always alone." She sank onto the bed. "There was no one else. Only me."

"Did you know he'd taken the map?"

Tears spilled down her cheeks. "Not until he showed it to me. He had it in his pocket. He said he liked to keep it close to his heart because it reminded him why he was really here. For love." She broke into sobs. "But I was so overcome with jealousy that I couldn't think straight. The thought of Higgins with someone else..." She pressed her palms flat against her temples. "I couldn't bear it."

"And when he denied there was someone else, you didn't believe him?" I prompted.

She shook her head. "I thought he had her stashed away somewhere. That the map only proved his deceit. They were going to hunt for the treasure together, to fund their new life. I was furious that he would lie to me."

Talk about paranoid and neurotic. "Did he know how you felt about him?"

"I never told him explicitly," Laura said. "I couldn't. I had to act indifferent. He was the butler, you see. Mommy adored Higgins, but she would've cut me off had she known."

"But she's dead now," I said. "You were free to choose."

"And that's why I decided to out myself, but when I went to Mommy's estate, Higgins announced he was heading to Starry Hollow for a few days. I convinced myself there was someone else. That only another woman could lure him away from me in my time of need." She sniffed. "I'd never felt good enough for him. I pictured him with some devoted brownie. A woman who could take care of him in a way that I couldn't."

I handed her a tissue from the box on the bedside table. Streaks of mascara appeared under her eyes. All the magic in the paranormal world and she couldn't find a decent water-proof mascara.

"I loved him beyond reason," she said, blowing her nose. "He was so shocked to see me in the bathroom." She reached for more tissues.

"And you didn't know how Higgins felt about you?" I asked.

"Sometimes I thought I detected a look in his eye, but he was Higgins," she said. "The butler. He never would've compromised his position."

"But your mother's death seems to have prompted him to take action," I said. "I think he felt like it was now or never."

Laura stared at the vials on the dresser. "Never, apparently." She inhaled deeply. "He tried to tell me the truth, but I was already so angry. He showed me the map and said that he'd hoped to find the treasure and offer it to me as a gift. Like a knight bringing back the head of a dragon for his princess."

"He wanted to prove he was worthy of you," I said softly.

"He didn't need a treasure for that," Laura said. "He'd earned my love a long time ago and I rewarded him by burying a corkscrew into his gut. I was so horrified, I ran from the bathroom before he even had time to collapse."

"He didn't collapse," I said. "Not in the bathroom, anyway. He came looking for help." I paused. "Why did you take the map?"

"I don't know," she said. "It fell on the floor when I…when I…" She couldn't say the words. "It was instinct. When I got back to my hotel, I noticed the blood on it and freaked out. I threw it away before I got back to my room."

"There were no fingerprints on the corkscrew," I said. "How is that possible if you ran from the bathroom so quickly after stabbing him?"

"I held the corkscrew in the edge of my sleeve because it looked grubby. I didn't want to touch it with my bare hand." She wrinkled her nose. "Gross." Her attention returned to the vials. "I should never have run off. I should have stayed and used it on myself."

"Laura, I understand how you might feel right now, but please don't do anything rash."

She drew her knees to her chest. "Why not? It's either die now, or rot in prison for the rest of my life. And I deserve the worst possible fate."

"You seem a little…" How could I say it without setting her off? Unhinged? Mentally unbalanced? "You seem to be struggling. Maybe your lawyer can set you up with a psychiatrist. I don't know about the paranormal world, but, in the human world, there are certain defenses available." Was that justice for Higgins, though? I didn't know. What I did know was that, by all accounts, Higgins was the type of man who would have shown her mercy. He wouldn't want Laura to suffer, not if he truly loved her.

Laura squeezed her arms around her knees. "I think I would prefer to join Mommy and Higgins in Nirvana."

I sat beside her on the bed. "Why are you still here, Laura? You could have downed those vials days ago. Or you could have fled the country. You have enough money to hide for the rest of your life."

"I don't know," she whispered. "Higgins is still here. I guess I couldn't bear to leave him behind."

"We never really leave behind those we love," I said. "We carry them with us wherever we go."

She sniffed. "He was so good and kind. He always looked out for me. When I was a little girl, I told my mother that when I grew up, I was going to marry Higgins." A small smile formed on her lips. "Mommy laughed and said I'd feel differently when I was older, but I never did."

I took out my phone. "I'm going to call the sheriff now. I don't want you to touch those vials. Higgins wouldn't want that, either."

Laura nodded absently. "He was so good and kind." She buried her face between her knees. "So good and kind. You didn't deserve him, Laura. You deserve to rot."

My heart ached for both Higgins and Laura. They both felt unworthy of the other's love and now they would never get the chance to overcome it.

"Sheriff, I'm here with Laura Stanhope," I said. "She has a few things to tell you. I'm going to drive her over to your office now." I paused to listen as he ranted and raved about my lunacy in handling her alone when he told me to wait. I held the phone away from my ear as he ordered me to call hotel security and sit tight until he got there.

When I finally ended the call, Laura leaned her head on my shoulder. "He loves you, you know. I could hear it in his tone. So frantic. How lucky you are." Her voice was practically a whisper.

I swallowed hard. "To be honest, he's good and kind, and I don't know that I deserve him, either."

"What will happen to the map?" she asked. "Will it go to Uncle Larry now?"

"It will get logged into evidence," I said. "Beyond that, I'm not sure."

"Life is very tiresome," she said. "I shall be grateful for the rest in prison."

The door burst open and two security guards crowded the entryway.

"Nobody move," the first guard said.

"Not to worry, my turtle doves," Laura said. "We're waiting for the sheriff to arrive. There's nothing more attractive than a man doing his duty. Trust me on this."

CHAPTER 17

"Remind me why we need to bring backup to a gingerbread house?" the sheriff asked. "The murder's been solved." We stood outside Bewitching Bites with Deputy Bolan, Linnea, and Aster.

"I don't think they'll remember us," I said. "But we need to find out what they're hiding." It may not have been connected to the murder, but there was something suspicious about the Gerstbergers. "Whatever you do, don't eat anything in the shop. Not a nibble."

"Seems a shame," the sheriff said, admiring the delicious-looking exterior.

Linnea examined the outside. "I feel like I've been here before."

"You may have been," I said. "They don't like customers to remember."

"What an odd way to do business," Aster said. "The boys have asked to come in here on occasion when we've passed by, but I've always said no."

"That's because you have good instincts," I said.

We entered beneath the arched candy canes. Hedy and

Hannah were behind the display cases, arranging a tray of chocolate unicorn horns that sparkled with gold flecks. I stiffened when they looked at me, but their smiles reflected their absent memories.

"Welcome to Bewitching Bites," Hedy said. "How lovely to have a large group. Won't you try a sample of our golden apples?"

"Not today," I said, and nodded to my cousins. "Work your magic, witches."

Linnea directed her attention to Hedy, and Aster to Hannah. With the flick of an elegant finger, the Gerstbergers were immobile except for their mouths.

"Tell us why you didn't want the sheriff to remember his visit," I said.

"The sheriff was here?" Hedy asked. "When?" She seemed genuinely baffled.

The sheriff walked over to them. "I can ask my own questions, Rose." He chewed his lip, studying Hedy Gerstberger. "What is it you didn't want me to remember? The minotaur made of gold? The fact that you have ledgers dating back hundreds of years? What secret are you hiding?"

Hedy's eyes were wild, not with anger, but fear. What was she so frightened of?

"I can't tell you," she choked.

"I think you have *can't* confused with *won't*," I said. "Didn't you learn grammar rules in school?" I clucked my tongue. "Kids today."

"Okay, Rose," the sheriff said, easing me aside. "Hedy, do you always make customers forget they've been here?"

Hedy remained silent.

"No," Hannah interjected. "Not always. It depends."

We turned our attention to the daughter.

"Be quiet, Hannah," Hedy hissed.

"Mother, we need to tell them," Hannah insisted. She looked awkward, her body stiff except her moving mouth.

"It's a family secret, Hannah," her mother said. "We can't break with tradition. It simply isn't done."

"Now you sound like my mother," Linnea said. "Have I mentioned how much my mother gets under my skin?"

"I'm very uncomfortable," Hedy complained. "Could you please undo the spell?"

"Not until we've finished our conversation," Sheriff Nash said. "We can't trust you not to shove magical candy in our mouths and send us on our merry way."

"If you ate the candy, it was of your own free will," Hedy said. "We can't force anyone to eat."

"That's why I managed to get out," I said. "They tried to insist, but that was as far as they could get."

Hedy tried to shift her gaze to me. "You resisted?"

"Wasn't easy," I said. "I love chocolate with the passion of a million Harry Potter fans."

Everyone frowned at me.

"Human world reference," I said. "It just means I really love chocolate."

"I'm going to put these handcuffs on you," the sheriff said, nodding to Deputy Bolan. "Then the witches are going to undo the spell."

"We're under arrest?" Hannah asked, panic flooding her voice.

"First, you're going to take us on a tour of your facility," the sheriff said. "Show us your secrets."

"And if you try anything foolish," Linnea said, holding up a finger. "Well, just don't try anything foolish."

Deputy Bolan ran behind the women and cuffed them. Then my cousins undid their respective spells.

"Let's go," the sheriff prodded them.

We followed the women to the backroom where a full

kitchen was in use. Two large ovens. Two long wooden tables. A caddy with rolling pins and other baking tools. A spiral staircase was visible in the back corner of the room.

"What's downstairs?" I asked.

"Where we store the chocolate," Hedy answered quickly. Too quickly.

"Why do you store it there?" the sheriff asked. "What's wrong with in here?"

"Temperature's better down there," Hedy said.

The sheriff guided her toward the staircase. "Show me."

"We'll wait here with Hannah," Aster said.

I joined Hedy and the sheriff on the spiral staircase. It seemed a long way down, much further than a basement.

"Why did you come here?" Hedy asked on the march down.

"Your shop was listed on a map," the sheriff said. "The map is connected to a dead butler."

"A map," she repeated. "How old?"

"Not sure," the sheriff said. "Why?"

"We've been very careful," Hedy said. "An older map would indicate that one of our ancestors failed to protect what's ours. A treasure map, I presume."

"That's right," the sheriff said. "How'd you know?"

We reached the bottom of the staircase and the answer quickly became clear. The far side of the room was laden with treasure. Chalices, coins, statues—you name it, the Gerstbergers had it stored beneath their candy shop.

"This treasure has remained unmoved for centuries," Hedy said. "We've added to the collection over the years, whenever a pirate, or someone of great wealth, entered the shop. The royals were our favorite. They always carried such valuable items." She laughed softly. "Not on their person, of course, but their staff was always with them, carting around their expensive jewels and such."

I gestured to a delicate crown on a velvet cushion. "Like that?"

"That was taken right off the head of a fae queen," Hedy said proudly. "It's one of our most prized possessions."

"You stole these items," I said.

"Mostly from thieves," Hedy said. "The majority of the treasure is the ill-gotten gains of vampire pirates. Would you have us return them?"

"Maybe to their rightful owners," I said. "There's this amazing thing called the internet these days. You could probably track down a lot of the rightful owners."

"As though you wouldn't want to own a piece of history," Hedy said.

"What are you?" I asked. It had been bugging me that I couldn't tell the type of paranormals they were.

"They're shifters," the sheriff said, sniffing. "But I can't tell beyond that."

"We're raven shifters," Hedy said. "We don't shift in cycle with the moon, though. In fact, our kind rarely shift at all, anymore. Back when vampire pirates still roamed the seas, my family would fly out to monitor the docks for their arrival. Then we'd lure them into the shop, usually with a comely young maiden."

I shook my head. "Men are so easy."

"And you'd empty their pockets," the sheriff said.

"In exchange for our delicious chocolate," Hedy said. "We considered it a fair trade."

"Is there really a missing gold minotaur?" I asked.

"Oh, yes," Hedy said, with a puff of sadness. "It's the one that got away. I don't know what happened to it, but I consider it a great loss to our collection."

"I'm sure you do," I shot back. "Why are you afraid of losing the treasure? What happens?"

Hedy swallowed hard. "There's magic in this treasure.

Magic that has kept our family going for generations. Magic that keeps the gingerbread house standing. The shop didn't always look this way. It's fueled by magic."

"So remove the magic and the whole thing goes?" I queried.

"Hannah and I included," Hedy said.

"Why?" I asked.

Hedy closed her eyes. "Because the magic is keeping us going, too."

"How so?" I asked. They didn't strike me as particularly old.

"Because they lied, Rose," the sheriff said. "There haven't been generations of them. It's been the two of them from the beginning. Some of the magic in here keeps them from aging."

I stared at the treasure. "Like a fountain of youth?"

"We don't know which item is responsible," Hedy said. "We've tried to figure it out over the years but to no avail."

"So, you're actually the one responsible for Bewitching Bites ending up on a map," I said. "Not an ancestor."

"It was Hannah," Hedy said sharply. "She let a handsome man out of here years ago without making him eat. He caught a glimpse of our haul and, I believe, pocketed a few gold coins on the way out, and probably the minotaur as well, but Hannah was smitten with him and made me swear not to go after him."

"I'm surprised he didn't come back for more," I said.

"That may well have been his intention," Hedy said. "That's why maps were made and stashed away, so the treasure could be found later."

"Anytime someone asks questions, or feels like they've visited us before but can't quite remember, they're offered a sample," Hannah said. "We don't want anyone to remember us, not only because of the treasure, but because of *us*."

The sheriff took Hedy by the arm and directed her back to the staircase. "Thanks for telling your story, Hedy."

She craned her neck to look at the treasure. "What happens now?"

"Like Ember said, we'll try to track down the rightful owners of these pieces," the sheriff said. "And you'll be booked on multiple counts."

"We'll never make it to prison," Hedy said sadly. "Not if the treasure goes first."

"I'm sorry, Hedy," the sheriff said. "It seems to me you've had more than your fair share of time."

"What if she tries to shift once we're outside and flies away?" I whispered.

"Not in these cuffs," the sheriff said. "They're special, remember? They cut off magic, or keep a shifter from changing shape. They're designed for paranormals."

Yes, I remembered now. I'd seen them in action before. "Maybe I should get a pair of my own. Seems like they'd come in handy."

The sheriff glanced over his shoulder and grinned. "Not a chance, Rose."

"Is that yours?" Marley asked.

We were returning from a practice session with Firefly and I was still riding high from Marley's excellent progress. I was starting to suspect she had more Rose blood pumping through her veins than I did.

"Is what mine?" I followed her gaze to the cottage. Leaning against the front door was a deep green broomstick with a brown leather strap. A red ribbon was tied in a bow around the neck.

Marley ran ahead to investigate. "There's no tag."

No, there wouldn't be. One good look at the elegant

broomstick and I knew exactly who'd left it. I couldn't resist a smile.

"It's from Alec, isn't it?" Marley asked.

I opened the front door and carried the broomstick inside. "What makes you say that?"

"Sheriff Nash would have given it to you himself. Alec's the only one who wouldn't want to take credit for the gift."

I ruffled her hair. "You're so smart that it scares me sometimes."

Marley beamed. "Maybe this means you still have a chance."

My expression soured. "Let's not worry about that, Marley. I'd rather focus on the fact I have my own broomstick."

"I get a unicorn and you get a broomstick," she said. "Seems fair." Her eyes grew round and solemn. "You're not going to make me fly everywhere with you now, are you? Because I still don't like heights."

"I won't make you do anything you're uncomfortable with," I said.

Marley paused thoughtfully. "Maybe you should."

Huh? I wasn't sure I'd heard her correctly. "What?"

"I don't want to end up like Alec," she explained. "If he's uncomfortable, he bails."

That much was true. "Sweetheart, you and Alec are very different. For starters, you're a child."

"Alec was a child once," Marley said. "Maybe his parents never pushed him out of his comfort zone. Maybe he was allowed to retreat and never fully experience discomfort, so he never learned to work through it."

I heaved a sigh. "I love how your brain works, I really do. But Alec is a grown vampire. Whatever his past experiences, he chooses fear over opportunity every day. No one can change that except him."

Marley smiled. "Maybe you're helping him to change it. Little by little." She tapped the end of the broomstick.

It was too much to hope for. Besides, I was focused on Granger now. It wasn't fair to the sheriff to secretly pine for my emotionally stifled vampire boss.

"I think I'm going to take this for a quick practice session," I said. "I assume you don't want to join me."

Marley recoiled. "I'll take PP3 for a walk and watch from the ground." She grabbed his leash and hooked it to his collar.

I dropped my handbag onto the coffee table and tucked the broomstick under my arm. "It's so funny. I actually feel like a witch today when I'm on a broomstick. It's the only time I really feel that way."

We stepped back outside, into the bright sunshine.

"All you need is a black cat for the tip of your broomstick," Marley called after me.

Will I do? Raoul appeared between the hedges.

"Hey, look. My friendly neighborhood stalker. Want to go for a ride?" I asked.

I'm your familiar, he said. *Comes with the territory.*

I straddled the broomstick. "Hop on. There's plenty of room."

I commanded the broomstick into the air, with my trusty raccoon holding on for dear life.

Regrets, I have a few, he said, hanging upside down.

"Pretend it's a tree branch and you'll be fine."

I waved to Marley and PP3 on the front lawn of the cottage. In the woods behind the cottage, a flash of color caught my eye as my vampire boss moved stealthily along the path that led to the main road. I assumed he'd taken the back path so that no one from Thornhold would register his visit. When he glanced skyward, I pretended not to notice him. That was what he wanted, and the part of me that cared for him wanted to give him whatever he desired, even at my own expense. Never mind that intense feelings like ours had been Higgins' and Laura's undoing. Alec and I had declared an emotional detente and I had to learn to live with it. I knew I'd never go near Alec with a corkscrew, just like he'd never come near me with his fangs. If Holly was his choice, then I would support his decision because that's what you do when you care about someone.

With a final glance at Alec, I turned my broomstick back toward my beloved family and headed for home.

Thank you for reading **Magic & Mercy**! If you enjoyed it, please help other readers find this book so they can enjoy the world of Starry Hollow, too ~

1. Write a review and post it on Amazon.

2. Sign up for my new releases via e-mail here http://eepurl.com/ctYNzf or like me on Facebook so you can find out about the next book before it's even available.

3. Look out for **Magic & Madness**, the next book in the series!

4. Other books by Annabel Chase include the **Spellbound** paranormal cozy mystery series.

Curse the Day, Book 1

Doom and Broom, Book 2

Spell's Bells, Book 3

Lucky Charm, Book 4

Better Than Hex, Book 5

Cast Away, Book 6

A Touch of Magic, Book 7

A Drop in the Potion, Book 8

Hemlocked and Loaded, Book 9

All Spell Breaks Loose, Book 10

Printed in Great Britain
by Amazon